VOICES OF THE PRISM
An Anthology of LGBTQIA+ Voices

Edited by
Amber Bliss

Cover Art and Design by
Rashaa Al-Sasah

2022

VOICES OF THE PRISM
An Anthology of LGBTQIA+ Voices
Edited by Amber Bliss

West Warwick Public Library
1043 Main Street
West Warwick, RI 02893
www.wwpl.org

This project was made possible in part by a grant from the Rhode Island State Council on the Arts, through an appropriation by the Rhode Island General Assembly and a grant from the National Endowment for the Arts.

Acknowledgements

I want to thank our friends at the Rhode Island State Council on the Arts for their generous funding as well as their support of writing, including genre writing, as art, which is rarer than you'd think. I'd be remiss if I didn't thank my colleague and co-director of the press, Rashaa Al-Sasah, who works behind the scenes on most of these publications in the trenches of administration, problem solving, and design. A special thanks to Kristen Bezner, who swooped in and joined the library team with a very specialized editorial skill set in a stroke of unusually good luck. Finally, a huge thank you to all of the staff at the West Warwick Public Library who proofread and copyedited until their vision was blurry, as well as endlessly stepped up to cover desks and other tasks throughout the library while my attention was diverted on this project. These projects could not be done without you.

Contents

Fantasy

Holding Out for a Hero

For companion Pavel, managing quest scrolls and mending armor in the shadow of his handsome hero is the heart of the job, until a rogue's dastardly plot puts life and love on the line.

Gardens Gone

Surviving as a witch depends on repressing everything that you are, a mantra Mira hears daily from her mother. But an accidental connection with the pale girl at her new school makes Mira question if there is another way.

Contemporary

What's Easier

As if struggling with classes and classmates in a new school weren't enough, Jules has just spotted his childhood best friend hanging rainbow flyers around the school. The best friend he kissed and never said goodbye to. Can Jules find the courage to put things right?

> *When facing an unimaginable loss, one woman finds her way through grief with the power of unconditional love in the pages of a journal.*

Science Fiction

> *In the Town, everyone works to make ends meet and move on to the next thing—until the next thing comes back around.*

> *After eir latest mission ended with blood on eir hands, animal rescuer Maude tracks eir newest charge to an inhospitable planet of scorching heat and finds the burning shore is not as uninhabited as ey had thought.*

Horror

> *Erich, a German soldier, is no stranger to the horrors of war, but nothing can prepare him for an enemy that won't stay dead.*

How far will a former high school teacher caught in the grinding cogs of addiction go to feed his habit?

A mysterious caller gets more than they bargained for when they dial the wrong resident on Begonia Drive.

Introduction

Voices of the Prism is a project that is near and dear to my heart as it features a community I'm proud to be a part of. The LGBTQIA+ community is full of thoughtful, compassionate, creative people, and this anthology is no different. This is the WWPL's first publication project that did not include an extended workshop model with weekly classes and significant group work, but in the course of just four workshop sessions, I watched these authors connect on a very genuine level and offer each other insights from an impressive well of diverse experiences and perspectives. I had the privilege of working with each of these amazing authors both individually and in groups. I don't have the space here to tell you how dedicated they are to their work or how supportive they were with their peers, but if you take a look at their stories, you'll see that for yourself. The work within represents a huge range of genres and themes, but each piece displays a depth of human emotion—from love and humor to grief and despair—that resounds in all of us.

So, dear reader, I implore you to explore this collection of voices, many of them new to the public, and catch a glimpse of the incredible people behind the work. You won't be disappointed.

~AMBER BLISS
June 2022

Holding Out for a Hero

by
K. Parr

"Hey, Pavel! Running a little late today, huh?"

I arrive at the Quest Center in wrinkled black trousers and an unbuttoned gray tunic, panting. I double over to catch my breath, but it doesn't seem to matter that I ran straight here—the line of companions waiting for quests has wrapped around the building.

I glare down at Dimwurst, a gnome who's just ahead of me in line. He jeers as I get behind him, and I curse his alcohol tolerance. The only reason I'm late is because he drank me under the table last night. We went to Companion School together, and I don't think he's ever forgiven me for trouncing him in our downtrodden hero pep talk class. Buying me drinks—and keeping me talking for hours—must've been his form of petty revenge. Too bad I'm a sucker for free booze *and* endlessly praising my hero, Jaxon.

"Hope there are some quests left by the time you reach the counter," Dimwurst continues smugly.

I don't rise to the bait and instead amuse myself by counting the moles peppering his bald head. One, two, three…

"Sure would be shameful if you couldn't get your hero a quest," he says.

The line moves forward and we follow. I note no one has slid into place after me—I'm the last one. Dimwurst's words churn in my stomach, but I keep counting. Four, five, six…it's like they're multiplying before my eyes.

Dimwurst lets out a pitying sigh. "I wonder what would happen if all the quests ran out. What would Jaxon think?"

I clench my fists but keep my mouth shut. Dimwurst's just jealous Jaxon was paired with me instead of him. I can't help it that our test scores demonstrated the highest compatibility.

Frankly, Dimwurst *should* be jealous. Jaxon is the perfect hero. Our previous quest involved slaying an ogre, and oh, how majestic Jaxon looked—gleaming plate mail, dark skin glinting with sweat, black hair cascading over his shoulders, perfect white teeth bared as he swung his sword to lop off the creature's head.

Because I like to torture myself, I've pictured that moment over and over. Stupid brain. Why do I fixate on someone I can never have? And yet my fall for him was inevitable the instant he accepted a flower crown from a little girl he'd saved.

Tough and brawny, but also sweet and cute? I was doomed from the start.

The problem is that Jaxon will never see me outside of my role as his companion. Compared to him, I'm scrawny, pale, and plain-looking—barely interesting enough to warrant notice, let alone romantic interest. Of course, that's why I chose to go to Companion School and *not* Hero Academy (or the Institute of Villainy, for that matter).

As Dimwurst prattles on about the glorious quests he's claimed for his own hero, I finish counting his moles and start tallying the Wanted flyers pasted on the bulletin board outside the center. There are more than I remember, mostly thanks to several copies of a post warning folks to be on the lookout for a comically mustachioed "rogue kidnapper" sighted in a nearby town. He's definitely a graduate of the Institute of Villainy with a curlicue mustache like that.

Finally, we enter the Quest Center and face the long, curving counter that takes up half of the building. There are three stations, each with a pair of harried elven employees who trade off on interrogating companions about what they seek, then flitting in front of a massive wall of cubby holes to locate and extract a scroll that matches. These scrolls contain requested tasks from around the world, each sorted into categories of difficulty, distance, and length. As companions, our job is to select the best quest for our hero and prepare for the journey ahead by packing supplies, securing horses, patching armor, and doing whatever else is necessary.

I have yet to fail Jaxon in this most sacred companion duty, but with the line shrinking and the cubby holes visibly emptying, my palms sweat. Even the number of employees dwindles as the rush dies down. When it's Dimwurst's turn, there's only one elf left. Dimwurst shoots me a haughty grin as he saunters to the counter. I stop at the "wait here" mark on the floor and wish it wasn't purposely far back to prevent eavesdropping.

The last, lone employee—I suspect the one with the least seniority—doesn't bother to speak to Dimwurst before grabbing a scroll and shoving it at him. I would've laughed at the rude exchange if I didn't have a horrible, creeping suspicion that I knew the reason behind the brusqueness.

Dimwurst flaunts his scroll in my direction before disappearing outside, and in his wake the room falls silent. I approach the counter and crane my neck to see if there might be any scrolls hiding in the darkened slots behind the remaining elf. Before I can open my mouth to inquire, the employee ducks out of sight and returns with a sign they prop up in front of them.

OUT OF QUESTS. COME BACK TOMORROW.

No. This can't be happening.

I latch onto the counter in desperation. "Are you sure there's nothing?"

The elf pointedly taps the sign.

Dimwurst's words haunt me, and I clench my trembling hands into fists. Did he have something to do with this? If only *murdering him* was a quest that existed.

"What about piecing together a treasure map?" My voice lurches. "Collecting ingredients for a ritual? Locating a lost pet?" My head swims. This is the only Quest Center I'm registered to use. If I can't get a quest here, I can't get a quest anywhere.

The employee crosses their arms over their chest. "Come back tomorrow."

Numb, I stagger out of the Quest Center and trudge to the cottage outside of town that I share with my sister between quests. An idea springs to mind, and I all but break the door down as I shove inside. "Sandira! You must have a quest."

There's a yelp, then the shattering of glass. "You idiot!"

Like me, my sister's a redhead, and we both inherited our father's beak nose, although she has round glasses perched on hers. She glares over her lenses before bending down to clean up the jar of pine needles she dropped. I hurry over to assist, but she shoos me away. As I hover in the nook that serves as her apothecary, I scan the shelves cluttered with books, bottles, herbs, and measuring devices.

"Do you need more plants or oils or…clients?" *Please*, I think. She must have *something* we can do for her, even if it's only a basic task.

Sandira finishes scooping the jar's remains into a bin and stands with hands on her hips. "What are you talking about? I've got plenty of—"

A knock on the front door precedes the grand entrance of Jaxon, who sweeps inside like a beam of sunlight. As befitting a hero, he's decked out in a green brocade doublet, brown breeches over gray hose, and fur-lined leather boots—all beneath a shimmery-blue embroidered cloak. He grins, showing off his pronounced dimples. When he combs fingers through his tousled hair, my knees threaten to buckle.

By the gods old and new, he's beautiful.

"Good morning." He bows to each of us before gazing at me. "Sorry to barge in, but I haven't heard about our next quest yet."

In response, I drop to my knees. "There weren't any quests left. I'm sorry. I failed you."

"What?"

"There's nothing for us to do today." I hang my head.

A pause. "So…what does that mean, exactly?" he asks.

"I'm not sure." I wallow in despair while Jaxon uncharacteristically says nothing. It's all my fault. I could kick myself for falling prey to Dimwurst's scheme. I should've tackled him for the last quest when I had the chance.

Sandira's snort cuts through the gloom. "Are you saying neither of you knows how to take a day off?"

I glower at her. Since being partnered with Jaxon at the official ceremony two years ago, my life has been one mad dash after another with little rest in between. We might've slowed down before, but we've never just…stopped. I don't think I'm capable of stopping.

Jaxon drums his fingers on his thighs, clearly panicking.

"I've got errands to run," I blurt, then cringe. Jaxon is a hero. He shouldn't help me with my companion duties, especially since I planned to rush through them before departing for our next quest. "Never mind. They're boring. It's a waste of time for you." My laugh is tinny.

But Jaxon perks up. "No, that's it! I'll assist you. I may be crafted for speed, stealth, strength, and agility, but no matter is too trivial. I promise to ensure the proper completion of your errands."

He beams, and my belly swoops.

"Er, thanks." I get lost in his deep brown eyes, and I must be wearing a dopey expression because Sandira snickers. I shake myself out of it. "Right, yes. Let me get my list."

One of my greatest joys in life is crafting to-do lists and crossing off each item once complete. That's probably why being a companion suits me, and one of the reasons I opted for this career in the first place. I glance at the page I left on the kitchen table. "Are you sure?"

"Very." Jaxon offers me a hand.

I try not to shiver at the feeling of his calloused skin brushing against mine as I rise to my feet.

He ushers me ahead of him. "Lead the way."

And then we're off.

We can see and hear our first destination—Smith Alley—long before arriving. Smoke wafts from smithies on either side of the lane, and apprentices with sooty faces pump the bellows while blacksmiths holler orders. Their pounding hammers rattle my skull as we pass.

At the last smithy on the left, a curly-haired girl greets me before gasping at the sight of Jaxon. She ignores me—something I'm used to as a companion—and tells Jaxon she reforged his daggers that had been dissolved by a serpent's poison a few weeks back. She transfers the weapons to him, and he gives them a twirl that makes her clap.

"These are impeccable." He weighs them in each hand. "How did you recreate such exact detail, down to my father's initials?" Reverently, he caresses the engraved letters on the handles.

"Your companion drew us a picture and provided all the specifics. He insisted we not forget a single thing."

Jaxon turns to me with soft eyes.

Embarrassed, I cut in before he can offer thanks. "We appreciate your prompt service," I tell the girl.

"Remember us for next time." She winks at Jaxon, but he doesn't wink back as usual. Strange. Then again, this whole day is strange.

Jaxon hangs his new daggers on his belt as we depart. Back in the main thoroughfare, I cross off the first item on my list and consider the second.

"Look out!"

I register Jaxon's shout seconds before I'm tackled to the side of the road. I cry out at the painful impact and land hard on the ground, inches away from a speeding horse carriage that lost its driver. My head spins as I struggle to regain my breath. The next thing I know, I'm being rolled onto my back and Jaxon is leaning over me, forehead creased in concern.

"Are you all right?" he asks.

I'm too stunned to respond. Slowly I take stock of my body—nothing broken, but a few bruises—then nod. Jaxon takes my hand and helps lever me upright.

"Sorry about that." He wipes the dirt off my chest. "I didn't mean to push you so hard."

My pulse picks up, yet it has nothing to do with the almost-accident. This is far from the first time Jaxon's heroism has directly impacted me, but he's sitting so close I can feel the warmth radiating from him. I flail to my feet and clear my throat. "All good. You saved my life again. Thank you."

"Always." He retrieves the to-do list I dropped when I fell. "What's next?"

I accept the page from him. "I've got to pick up some foodstuffs for our next quest." Whenever *that* will be. Hopefully tomorrow.

"Sounds good. After you."

We head to the center of town where the market sprawls across a large cobblestone square. Merchants hawk their wares and oil sizzles as packs of shrieking children dart through the masses. The scent of spices is thick in the air, strong enough to make me sneeze. Behind a wagon a girl kneads dough with rhythmic slaps.

I aim for a stall on the outer ring, but Jaxon waylays me to drag me over to a section of clothing vendors. Colorful garments flap on clotheslines stretched between the carts as Jaxon skims his fingers across an array of fabrics spread on a table. He pauses on a green silk tunic with silver embroidery and pearl buttons. The merchant woman behind the table gives him a toothy grin.

Jaxon turns to me. "Is this not the smoothest material you've ever felt?"

Before I can protest, he places the finery in my hands. The soft fabric glides across my skin, and I agree.

"You should get it," he says.

I may get paid fairly well from Jaxon's spoils, but he's missing the point. This kind of flashy look is for a hero, not a companion. "I…don't think it suits me."

"Nonsense. The color brings out your eyes."

My heartbeat stutters. He's probably trying to set me up with someone else. That's all this is…right? But he's looking at me with a kind smile, his eyes crinkled at the edges. He shifts closer, and my words disappear as I inhale the heady smell of pine and campfire smoke.

Jaxon faces the merchant. "I would like to buy this, please." He pays the woman, then holds the garment out to me. "Here. You should try it on."

I'm frozen, but Jaxon is undeterred. Gently, he steers me to a changing tent beside the merchant's cart. Without asking, he joins me in the enclosed space. He lifts the tunic. "May I?"

I flush but manage a jerky nod.

Jaxon bunches up the tunic, then tugs it over my head.

I shudder in his embrace, so lightheaded I don't hear his next question. "Mm?" I murmur, incapable of normal human speech.

"I asked if you can raise your arms." There's amusement in his voice.

I force my limbs to cooperate and stand there with my arms ramrod straight like a scarecrow.

Jaxon bites back a laugh. "You'll need to bend your elbows."

Somehow we wrangle the tunic on. I mourn the loss of his proximity when Jaxon steps back to appraise me. He frowns, then undoes his belt.

"What are you—?" I choke as Jaxon reaches around me to secure the belt on my waist, complete with his daggers and full scabbard. Then he removes his cloak with a flourish and drapes it over me. When he finishes, he eyes me with a wide grin.

"You look like a proper hero now." He squints. "Actually…you need one more thing." He raises a finger. "Be right back!"

He darts out of the tent, and I stand there like a fool in a costume. What more is he getting for me? I don't know what he's playing at with this new companion dress-up game, but my poor heart can't take much more. I should stop this charade before it goes any further, but I decide to humor his latest mood so he can get it out of his system.

I wait and wait for Jaxon's return, but he doesn't reappear. Eventually, I'm forced to relinquish the changing tent to another customer. Outside, the sun confirms he's been gone longer than he said. A cold sense of foreboding sinks like a stone in my stomach. Jaxon may be absentminded at times, but not like this.

I zip into the crowd, Jaxon's weapons digging into my thighs as I pump my legs. He's tall, so I should spot him easily, but I don't see him. Where would he have gone? I retrace our steps and check a few of his favorite taverns to no avail. The only place I haven't searched is my cottage. Would he have gone there to fetch something for me?

Passersby give me curious looks as I burst into a run, but I ignore them. I trip over Jaxon's cloak twice—it's far too big for me, and too hot—but I catch myself and push onward. I need to make sure he's okay.

I throw open the door to my house, startling Sandira from near the window where she's reading a book in a rocking chair.

"Is Jaxon here?" I demand, breathless.

"No. Why?" Sandira frowns as she sets down her book and joins me.

"He's gone! He's just…gone." My shoulders slump.

"What happened?" She starts to put a soothing hand on my arm, then double-takes. "Why on earth are you dressed like that?"

"It's not important. I think something's wrong." I pace as I explain the situation. "He wouldn't have just disappeared, not without saying anything. He's not like that."

"Did you check your mailbox? Maybe he left you a message."

I suck in a breath. Right! Our official mailbox is in town, in the Adventurer's Post Office next door to the Quest Center. If something urgent came up, using our mailbox would be the most convenient way to share information safely and privately.

Sandira snags my sleeve before I can dash away. "I'm coming with you."

I offer her a small smile, grateful for the comfort. Without another word, we hasten into town. I skid to a halt in front of our mailbox in the post office and fumble the lock open with a key I keep chained around my neck. Inside, there are two pieces of folded parchment. One is a junk offer for horse insurance, and the other…I unfold the page with shaky hands. Over my shoulder, Sandira joins me in reading:

Greetings, Jaxon! I have taken your companion!
Come alone at sunset with 1,000 gold pieces, and I will
set him free without a scratch.
Misheed my words, and he dies.

On the back are directions for where to meet.

I stare blankly as if the words will rearrange themselves to make sense. This isn't possible. Then I glance down at myself, and terror sets in. A gaping void fills my head, consuming every thought except raw fear that Jaxon will be killed. Killed because he dressed me up to look like him, and in a world where thousands of hero-companion pairs venture on quests every day, some idiot mistook the two of us.

Ignoring the rest of the post office occupants, I tear at my clothes—Jaxon's clothes—as if I could reverse what's happened. I hate that Jaxon is out there alone and weaponless, thanks to me.

There is a ray of hope, though. If the person who captured Jaxon believes him a weak companion, they might underestimate him. Jaxon has a number of charms and wiles, and I've seen him wrestle a bear and win. He's strong, even without his sword and daggers.

Unless they're torturing him.

A hysterical laugh bursts from my lips. We got a quest after all, but it's wrong. I'm only a companion. I can't save Jaxon.

Sandira claps a hand over my wrist, stilling me. "What are you waiting for? Go after him!"

"But how? I'm not…"

"What, a hero?"

I nod and want to crumple into a pathetic ball on the floor. I've trained for years to be a companion. While Jaxon learned battle strategies, I learned how to efficiently distribute the weight in our saddlebags. While he became skilled in hand-to-hand combat, I memorized what combinations of soap to use to get bloodstains out of tough fabrics. I know how to stitch socks, cauterize wounds, skin rabbits, prepare stew.

I don't know the first thing about mounting a rescue mission.

A prick of pain distracts me from my downward spiral. I rub the sore spot and glare at Sandira, who'd pinched me. "What was that for?"

Instead of answering, she pinches me again.

"Ow, quit it!"

"Get over yourself," she says. "You can do it."

"You really think so?"

"You've been working with him long enough. What would he do in your situation?"

A lump forms in my throat. She's right, and it's not a hypothetical question, since Jaxon's rescued me countless times—including earlier today. In Companion School, I learned how to be distracting and stall for time to give the hero the chance to swoop in. Maybe I can use some of those tactics to my advantage.

I swallow. I owe it to Jaxon to try.

"Thank you," I tell my sister. I inventory everything on me, and a plan begins to form. "I need to get my rucksack. Do you have any potions to spare?"

Sandira's grin is wicked, and her eyes glint. "Oh, I might have a few."

We race back to the cottage. I seize my rucksack and fill it with rocks until it's difficult to lift. I hope the bag looks heavy enough to weigh 1,000 gold pieces. Meanwhile, Sandira prepares a bandolier of colorful potions and powders that she drapes across my chest. She describes the contents of each corked vial, but the information doesn't stick to my frazzled mind. I figure it doesn't matter. I'm confident that whatever I grab will be helpful because my sister is excellent at her job.

"Are you sure I can't go with you?" Sandira asks when she finishes.

I give her a quick peck on the cheek. "I'm sure." She has never encountered danger in her life and I don't want that to change. *I'm* the companion, the one who chose to charge into battle and fight deadly beasts and traverse perilous roads—all on Jaxon's heels, of course. Jaxon and I are partners, promised to aid one another through thick and thin.

He is *my* responsibility, just as I am his.

I take a bracing breath then bound into the fading afternoon light.

The kidnapper chose a secluded spot in the woods, several miles from the town where the road becomes an arched rock bridge over a rushing river. The sun has reached the horizon by the time I arrive, huffing and puffing. On the opposite shore, Jaxon's kneeling on the ground, tied up and gagged. A lanky white man in black hose and a black tunic holds a knife to his throat. The man's stance is confident—clearly he's done this before—and a scar bisects the right half of his face. At the curlicue mustache poking from beneath shaggy brown hair, I gasp in recognition.

The kidnapping rogue from the Wanted posters. I should've known.

There's a cut oozing blood on Jaxon's forehead and his gaze appears glassy. When he notices me, his eyes widen and he lets out a muffled sound that earns him a sharp cuff to his temple. I stifle a cry as he crumples to the side.

The rogue laughs. "I'm glad you've come, hero. I wondered if this village was worth my time until I saw your companion here." He kicks Jaxon in the side, and I blanch when Jaxon cries out in pain.

"He's awfully well-dressed," the rogue goes on. "That made me realize just how much you care about him. And how much you might be willing to pay to get him back." He leers, his gaze on the sagging rucksack I'm struggling to keep on my back.

Mustering my courage, I run to the middle of the bridge and strike what I hope is a heroic pose, though the heavy bag throws me off-balance. "How DARE—?" My voice breaks. I cough and start over, "How *dare* you injure my…my companion! You said you wouldn't even scratch him. No way can I pay the full amount when you've clearly gone back on your deal."

The rogue rubs his stubble then adopts a mockingly contrite expression. "Ah. My apologies. It was difficult to resist. Your companion's quite mouthy. He must drive you mad."

"On the contrary, I love what my her—my companion says. Every word."

Jaxon uncurls and fixes me with a look I can't interpret.

The rogue appears disinterested as he spins his knife. "Just give me the money so I can continue on my way. I have other people to kidnap." He steps toward me.

I flounder, but an idea strikes. With a grunt, I heft the rucksack onto the side of the bridge. "If you want the money, you'll have to get it!" I shove the bag over the edge, and it splashes into the water with a loud *plop* before disappearing beneath the swirling current.

The rogue doesn't go after the bag.

I did not think this through.

The rogue scowls. "What did you do that for? Don't you get how a hostage exchange works? For a hero, you're not very smart."

I bite my tongue on a retort. He's certainly one to talk about lacking intelligence. You'd think he'd notice the stark physical differences between myself and Jaxon and realize his error, but alas.

"What, no monologue?" he demands. "What kind of hero are you?"

I can't give up the ruse. Jaxon is counting on me.

I wrack my brain for the impressive speeches Jaxon's performed over the past few years—he aced monologuing in Hero Academy. "Have you heard of my…my prowess in battle?" Not the best start, but the rogue's gaze is locked on me. Good. If I can keep him occupied, Jaxon can utilize his hero skills to escape. Hopefully. I can't exactly check if I want to keep the rogue's attention on me.

The rogue lifts an eyebrow. "Oh?" He strolls onto the bridge, knife outstretched and a malicious smirk on his face.

I scramble to draw Jaxon's sword, but it gets snagged in the scabbard. Sweat runs down my back as I tug, but my fingers have lost all feeling.

"I'm waiting for your story, hero. Well?"

I try not to think about how slowly he's moving, as if stalking prey—me.

I recall Jaxon's daggers, but as I reach for them, I graze the bandolier. A better plan emerges.

"I'm strong," I say. "S-smart. Stealthy." I pry a vial of purple liquid free from a slot and raise it threateningly. "Don't come any closer, or you'll be sorry!"

The rogue, halfway to me at the midpoint of the bridge, pauses. He wrinkles his nose. "You're not even going to fight me properly? What a waste." He shakes his head and mutters to himself, "Can't even find a proper nemesis around here."

When he turns to go back to Jaxon, I lob the vial at him with a shout. The rogue spins around and curses, but my aim is poor. The vial smashes against the far side of the bridge, nowhere near him. A pool of purple spreads around the glass fragments, smoking faintly.

He sneers. "Have you ever even killed *anything*?"

"Of course I have." I frantically feel for another vial. "Um. Dragons! I've defeated them. Loads of them."

"You?" He gives me a once over. "*You*?" His tone drips with sarcasm.

"Yes. I was t-top of my class. I've done so many amazing things…you couldn't even guess!" I hurl a vial of white powder at him. Or try to. I'm sweating so badly that when I wind my arm back, the vial slips from my grasp and actually lands several feet behind me. The glass doesn't break but it does crack, and a dusty cloud trails out of the jagged opening.

The rogue's face darkens. "Okay, now you're just pissing me off. Let me do this world a favor and put you out of your misery." In a move too quick to follow, he stows his knife and pulls out a shortsword. How the heck was he concealing such a weapon?!

Before I can contemplate the answer, he charges up the bridge.

In a blind panic I claw at the bandolier and fling whatever vials I can free in time, which isn't many. Of the three, two drop to the dirt and harmlessly roll away, their contents safely intact. The third strikes the earth hard enough to shatter. A nearly transparent substance oozes out several paces in front of me, stinking of licorice.

The pathetic volley of vials doesn't deter the rogue, who licks his lips in menacing anticipation as he nears striking distance. With my heartbeat thudding in my ears, I stumble backward but my foot slips on something hard and round. I crush the rest of the second vial as I topple to the ground in a tangle of limbs. I've fallen perpendicular to the road, my body wedged sideways and completely blocking the way. On my back, arms and legs spread wide, my eyes sting as I blink into a cloud of white dust.

That's when I realize I can't move.

And *that's* when I realize it's not dust—it's Sandira's white powder, otherwise known as paralysis powder.

I only have a second to process this before there's a strangled yelp. Only my eyes can move, so when I strain them to the side, I witness the rogue step one boot into the transparent substance and lose all control of his movement. With windmilling arms and a terrified expression, he barrels into me at full speed. I gasp at the fresh agony in my ribs while his toes hook under my prone body and his momentum sends him flying down the other side of the bridge, head over heels. His pained grunts warble through the air in sync with his somersaults before he crashes and the area goes quiet and still.

My harsh breathing fills the silence until a familiar voice speaks up.

"Pavel, are you okay?"

I would've swooned if I wasn't already lying flat on the ground.

Jaxon looms over me, since he's apparently freed himself from his bindings as expected of a hero. He's the most beautiful thing I've ever seen, all sweaty and worried, and I can't stop myself—not with the amount of adrenaline coursing through my veins.

"Gods, I'm so in love with you," I blurt, and then cringe.

Good to know the paralysis powder also didn't affect my jaw or tongue.

Jaxon's eyes widen, and I want to snatch the words back even though it's too late.

"Ah, never mind! Don't listen to me." I do my best to glance toward where the rogue had vanished from view. "What happened to him?"

Jaxon stares at me for a moment longer before peeking at the rogue. "Looks like he fumbled and hit his head on a rock."

"Oh. Good."

"What about you?" Jaxon returns his attention to me. "Can you move?"

I can't even shake my head. "No. It's paralysis powder," I say. "Don't know how long it'll last. My sister can fix it if you get me to her."

He nods, a serious look on his face, and I'm struck by the absurdity of this whole situation. I burst into a fit of uncontrollable giggles. "Want to hear something funny?" I babble. "I filled my favorite rucksack with rocks and now it's at the bottom of the river! What was I thinking, huh?"

"Hey, shh. It's okay."

Gentle hands cradle my head, and Jaxon's thumbs sweep away tears as my manic laughing transforms to sobbing. I'm clearly not cut out to be a hero, and I may not even get to be a companion anymore, not if Jaxon is offended by my stupid confession. Maybe he'll end up with Dimwurst after all, if the switch gets approved.

What have I done?

"Pavel? Come on, I've got you. You're safe, I promise. Can you look at me?"

I've never heard Jaxon speak so softly before. It snaps me out of my crying until we're gazing into each other's eyes. Even when I sniffle, Jaxon doesn't look away.

He swallows. "Um. I just. Wanted to say…" Pink tinges his cheeks. "I—"

A loud groan comes from the direction of the rogue, and Jaxon sighs. "Hold on a minute." He releases me, and a moment later, there's a thud and it's quiet again. Jaxon takes up his earlier position with his hands framing my jaw, warm and soft. "Where was I?"

"I…have no idea." I feel floaty, my body distant.

"Right." Jaxon tucks a stray curl behind my ear, his expression so fond my heart constricts. "You're brave and clever, wise and caring." He takes my hand and squeezes. I wish I could squeeze back, but my limbs remain immobile.

"I wouldn't be the hero I am without such a loyal companion," he continues. "I'm in your debt." He bites his lip, then meets my gaze with an expression I've never seen. It's a mixture of fear and hope and wonder. And…and…

"I'm in love with you too," he says at last.

Jaxon's words wash over me in a tidal wave. "Jaxon," I breathe, too stunned to say anything else. I must be dreaming, or maybe I died. Am I truly alive in a world where my hero loves me back—me, a companion?

Doubt shadows Jaxon's face. "Is that…okay?"

Fresh tears well and spill down my cheeks. "Yes. More than okay."

Jaxon's dazzling smile lights up the area like sunlight through clouds. My cheeks hurt, and I realize I'm beaming back just as wide.

Jaxon sits me up and leans me against him as he rummages in his pockets. He produces a crumpled flower crown and does his best to smooth it out before he sets it on my head.

"There," he says. "A true hero."

Ah, so that's what he'd left to retrieve to complete my outfit.

I'm nearly vibrating with how badly I want to throw my arms around him, hold him close and breathe him in, but Sandira's powder is too potent.

Jaxon seems to sense my frustration and saves me from my predicament by bending to press his lips against mine. Our first kiss is awkwardly rigid on my part, which I blame on the paralysis, but it's also hot and wet and perfect.

Perfect like Jaxon, who is my hero while I am his companion—in more than one way.

And tomorrow is another day, another quest.

One that we'll conquer together.

Gardens Gone

by
A.M.H. Devine

The stench of truck exhaust, chewed gum, and concrete drifted through the open window of our apartment, and somehow that was a welcome change from the usual smell of dust in the walls. I took a deep breath of the city just as Mom closed the window and pulled the blinds shut.

"Are you hungry?"

She faced me with her lips pinched into a thin smile. Heavy bags hung under my mother's eyes, and the green of her irises had dulled to almost gray since we hid ourselves here. Even her skin, which had been kissed golden under the sun in our garden back home, looked pallid and dry. I wanted to ask her why she looked thirty years older than she had last month, but we'd barely spoken since moving in. You couldn't jump from silence to the question that towered over us both like a mountain.

Mom served me a plate of rock-hard toast that scraped at my throat as I forced it down.

"So," she said, sitting across from me. "New school."

"Mhm."

"Are you excited?"

She hadn't tried this hard since before the mob. Before my mistake. One day we were living happily in our cottage, gardening together every day before she'd play piano for me as I fell asleep, and the next day an angry crowd of people from the town was slamming fists into our door. They didn't say what they'd do to us then, but they promised they'd come back with lighters and gasoline if we weren't gone by morning. My fear felt like needles and my anger felt like drums as I hid behind my mother, no better than a child. Our little cottage stood empty the next day, and so did she.

All because I showed a girl I had magic.

We hadn't talked about it since. We hadn't talked about much of anything.

I swallowed another mouthful of toast and it felt like eating knives. "I guess more…nervous than anything. Obviously."

"Why would you be nervous?"

Her voice was strained, almost distorted. It sounded like it came from an old radio. That thin smile hadn't left her face, but the lines around her eyes hardened as she focused on me. Was this a test? As I groped blindly for what she wanted me to say all I heard was the yelling from the mob back home. A now familiar pang of guilt stabbed at my chest.

"I mean…it's my first day and everyone else has been in school for months. So I won't know anyone. And…." My voice dropped to a whisper. "And I don't want it to happen again."

Her smile vanished. "It won't happen again."

The words fell like stones on the table. I wanted to believe that she meant to comfort me, but there wasn't any warmth in her voice. The words were cold and firm, binding me like manacles to the truth that existed in her head.

I couldn't bear to meet her gaze anymore, so I looked to the wilted potted plant in the middle of the table. It had been a little jade succulent once. I'd given it to Mom for her birthday a few years ago. I picked it out because its pot was glazed a beautiful, speckled purple, and the plant itself was sad and wilted past any ordinary gardener's ability to revive. Mom wrapped her hands around the pot and beamed when I presented it to her, and the room filled with the thrum of magic as she closed her eyes and brought it back to life. The stem straightened and bulged with a second chance, the leaves uncurled and swelled with water and the purest green I could imagine. It was the same shade of green as her eyes. Her face was full of so much joy as she set the pot down on our cottage kitchen's windowsill.

"What a wonderful gift, to bring something beautiful back to life," she had said.

That plant was the only living thing other than us to make it out of the cottage. I had been the one to grab it on our way out. Just like Mom, its leaves had taken on a gray sheen since coming here. The city didn't suit it.

"Mom—"

"There's nothing to be nervous about." I felt the finality of the period at the end of her sentence. She went to work washing the dishes and pulled the blanket of silence back over us both. I considered walking out the door, but the prospect of endless weeks of unspoken grief and guilt hanging over us like a guillotine stood in my way.

"We need to talk about it," I said.

She looked as if I had poured ice water over her head.

"I know you blame me for what happened."

"I don't blame you, Mira."

"Then why won't you *look* at me?!"

She whipped around. "I'm doing my best. And I need the same from you. What happened at the cottage *won't* happen again here because we are not witches here, Mira."

I threw my hands into the air. "What does that even mean? Of course we're witches."

"Not here. Not anymore."

"Really? Can not-witches do this?"

As I reached out for the potted plant with my hands, I focused on the pool of bright, verdant energy at my core that had hummed there for as long as I could remember. I hadn't touched it since that day behind the schoolhouse. It felt like moss under bare feet and whispered through my head like leaves in a fresh spring breeze as I called it forth. My body sang with the energy as I imagined roots stretching down and fresh stems reaching up into new, joyous growth for this sad little plant. Just to remind her what we both could do.

Before my fingers could brush its leaves, Mom's talon-like hands snatched my wrists together. She bared her teeth at me like a wild dog, and for a moment I didn't recognize her. A ripple of fear streaked up my spine as my magic receded.

She must have seen the fear in my face, because she dropped my wrists like they burned her.

"Don't ever do that again," she said. The steel edge to her voice and stare didn't go anywhere. "Not here, not at school, not anywhere. You're old enough to know what the consequences are if you get caught."

A trial in front of this city's branch of the Witchcraft Regulation Authority, if we were lucky. If we were found guilty, I'd get taken to a WRA reformatory school and she'd get prison for life. Witches were found dead in ditches from time to time. No one asked questions about it because no one needed to. Those were the unlucky ones.

I nodded.

She took a steadying breath and swallowed the conversation like a thick, dry pill. "We won't be discussing this again. Now get to the bus. You're going to be late."

Bitter silence returned as I left and locked the door between us.

The sky outside was gray and heavy with the first hints of winter. A few brown leaves clung to the spindly trees growing from patches of dirty soil framed by cracked sidewalk. When we first moved here, I played a game with myself where I counted the cigarette butts on the ground. If I counted more than the day before, I lost. Today, I just kicked at any I saw instead. Maybe repeatedly bashing my toe against the cement would clear my head and free me from the lingering hold of Mom's icy glare.

It didn't work. All I got was a scuffed shoe and a sore foot from kicking the corner of the bench at the bus stop too hard.

The appraising, hungry eyes of a middle-aged man on the bus didn't make things better. He wore a heavy coat that settled around his thickset frame like a turtle shell, and his skin had a scaly, yellow quality that was just as reptilian. The longer we sat there the more I expected him to pull his head inside his jacket, but he was entirely still and entirely focused on me. I tried to keep my head down and make myself small, but his stare bored into me the whole time. I risked a glance up to see how close I was to the high school, and he struck at the opportunity.

"Pretty girl like you needs to be careful this time of year," he said in a raspy, cigarette-smoke voice. "All sorts of bad folk out there in the dark, looking to do no good."

I grimaced and looked back down at my scuffed shoes.

"Witches love getting their claws on pretty girls like you."

I wondered how he would react to the feeling of plants growing inside him. Kids used to joke that you shouldn't swallow watermelon seeds because watermelons would start growing out your navel. To them it had been a silly word of warning, but since I heard it I couldn't stop imagining how terrible that could be. And how easy it would be to make it happen. Maybe the vines wouldn't burst out his stomach, but I imagined them creeping up his throat to suffocate him. Maybe curling out his mouth and nose and wrapping around his neck for good measure.

A gray tongue flashed across his lower lip.

If I just had a watermelon seed…

We're not witches here.

I ground my teeth together and let out a shaky breath. I should be used to people like him by now. This was exactly the kind of person that would call up the city hotline and have my mother and me standing before a court in less than a day. He gurgled out a chuckle, and I hoped he couldn't see the poison writhing in my body, barely held back. I dug my nails into my palm and forced myself to focus on being normal, being a not-witch.

We lapsed back into silence until he got off at the next stop. I caught his eye through the window as the bus pulled away, and he flashed me a sharp, yellow smile before fading from view.

I hated this city. I hated the way people looked at me. They didn't even know I was a witch, but they still looked at me like I was either something to eat or something to hide. I hated that the gray from the concrete seemed to be seeping into Mom's skin, and I hated that it would probably end up happening to me too. I hated how hated we were. The weight of it pressed down on me all the time in the mistrustful eyes of strangers on the street. It radiated out from the WRA-sanctioned billboards lining the major highways, covered in pithy slogans about keeping your family safe by keeping witches under control. Because obviously all witches were out to enchant you, steal your money, and corrupt your children. What a joke.

Witches had been around long before Salem, but it wasn't long after that this stupid country decided they didn't want us here anymore. The Witchcraft Regulation Authority was founded as a way to keep people from taking matters into their own hands. Not like it did much, though. In cities, things had quieted enough over the years that we didn't have to worry so much about getting burned at the stake. The same couldn't be said for more isolated communities.

Did they burn our cottage after we left? Was the garden still there at all?

The brakes of the bus screeched, and we were in front of the high school.

The school back home in our little town had been small, almost nonexistent, compared to the cinderblock monstrosity before me now. A weathered stone fence ran around my old high school building, lining a lush grass yard and guarding the historic building that we gathered in each day. Here, mossy stones and sun-warmed grass were replaced with cracked concrete and a rusted chain-link fence. Old chip bags and bits of plastic littered the base of the fence like scattered seeds. Maybe if I tried my magic on them a garbage tree would grow and cover the school in a canopy of shopping bags and broken razors. The thought almost made me laugh.

I stepped through the gate in the fence and a current of students rushing to make the first bell pulled me in like a riptide. I caught snippets of conversations about upcoming science tests and rumors about who graffitied the school seal outside the principal's office, reminders that this was a normal day for everyone else. It was late October, and the school year was already marching on in its inescapable rhythm. All these people knew each other, or were at least known enough to not be a mystery. Now eyes tracked me as I followed the signs to the admin office, and whispers hemmed me like a shadow.

"Who is that?"

"She's kind of cute."

"Dude, shut up."

"Why does she look sick?"

I clenched the straps of my backpack. Did I look sick? Since entering the building I had definitely felt nauseous. Waves of *newness* anxiety mixed with the sea of anger and guilt already roiling inside me, and I was certain I'd either vomit or pass out by the end of the day if they didn't stop muttering about me.

The hallways twisted on for what felt like an eternity of fluorescent lighting, old linoleum, and endless beige lockers. Why did they design this school like a labyrinth? My old school was one bright hallway lined with doors. You could navigate it blindfolded. Here, I was stumbling into the minotaur's lair with no string to guide me back out.

I didn't notice the body planted right in my path until it was a millisecond too late. I collided with a boy who must have been part brick wall. Even his face had a ruddy hue, made only more dramatic by the shock of red hair on his head. I couldn't even mumble an apology before the interrogation began.

"Whoa, slow your roll. What's your name?"

"Mira."

"I haven't seen you around, are you new?"

"I'm new."

He looked down at me with a calculating expression. I felt like a creature behind the bars of a zoo exhibit, but with even less space between us. I stepped back and he leaned forward.

"What grade?"

"Tenth."

"Nice." He raked his gaze over me and a sharp, acidic wave of revulsion rose in my throat. He was younger than the man on the bus by a few decades and he lacked all of the smoke-stained grime, but they were clearly the same breed of monster. Hunger echoed across both their faces—a hunger bred from boredom, not need. Visions of vines creeping out of his mouth and nose filled my mind's eye. Pavement-cracking pressure stirred in my gut and I knew I needed to get as much space between the two of us as I could. Now.

"Excuse me—"

I ducked under his elbow and smacked into another person. This time, the person toppled over as easily as a house of cards.

A thin, gangly girl in a simple gray dress sprawled on the floor. Loose, dark hair fell down her back and bangs brushed the top of her eyelashes. She had soft blue eyes and thin, stiff lips open in an expression of surprised irritation. She was beautiful in an ethereal kind of way.

The rising panic, the nameless boy, the lockers, and the bustle of students muted as I held a hand out to her. I didn't remember making the decision to help her up, but the force that held me there was as certain as gravity.

She narrowed her eyes as she considered my offered hand, but after a beat something in her expression shifted. Was this strange force pulling on her too?

As soon as her hand met mine, a white-hot bolt of pure, racing energy sliced through my body. We both gasped and jerked away. I half expected my palm to be smoking, but it looked the same as it had a moment before. Hers did too. Still on the floor, she gaped at me, and my stomach plummeted into free fall.

I did it again.

I didn't know how and I didn't know why, but that had to be magic. Nothing else short of a lightning strike could make my nerves light up like that. I knew it, and it was clear she knew it too.

I charged down the hall. Maybe I'd get lucky this time. Maybe she wouldn't blab to the rest of the school community or report us to the WRA. Maybe nobody else, not even that stupid pig of a boy, saw it, or if they did they thought we just exchanged a bad static shock. That could happen in October, right?

My heart pounded so hard I thought it'd launch itself right out my chest by the time I made it to the admin office. A middle-aged woman with warm brown skin and a pair of very tiny glasses looked up at me from behind a pristinely organized desk.

"Are you Mira Scott?"

I nodded.

"Take a seat."

She talked me through my class schedule and a map of the building. She seemed like a kind person. I wanted to pay attention because I knew she was doing her best to make sure I didn't get lost again, but almost all of my attention was on the door to the office. I expected that girl to burst in at any moment screaming *witchcraft!* The minutes crept by and the bell rang, and still no vicious, public accusation.

The nice office woman patted me on the shoulder and ushered me off to class with a gentle smile.

I reached my first class just in time for the teacher to begin the new student public hazing ritual—the forced introduction. He had me stand at the front of the class and share one fun fact about myself. I wouldn't have been able to repeat what I said because I was so focused on scanning the room of curious faces, but the girl with blue eyes and cold shoulders wasn't there. The boy from earlier wasn't either. My heart rate slowed, but the dull pressure building behind my forehead wasn't easing any time soon.

"Mira?"

"Sorry, what?"

The teacher chuckled. "I'm hoping you won't be daydreaming like that during the rest of class. I was just asking where you and your family moved here from."

This school seemed determined to have me dance across a minefield today.

"Oh, just a small town a couple hours from here. Most people haven't heard of it. My mom, uh, got a new job. In the city." I imagined a cartoonish droplet of sweat running down the side of my face.

The teacher released me to my seat—thankfully in the back of the room—and I spent the remainder of the class period glancing at the door, glancing at the window, and predicting how furious Mom was going to be when she found out. Was I single-handedly sending her to a lifetime behind bars? I heard the reformatory schools weren't much better than prisons either. Maybe there were other witches here we could reach out to for help. I remembered Mom mentioning once years ago that sometimes witches were safe enough in cities to gather behind closed doors from time to time. Surely they knew how to handle situations like this.

If we could find them without getting ourselves killed.

Miraculously, I had no classes with the girl that morning. Each time I walked into a new room I felt like I was about to plunge into an icy lake, and the only hope for air was not seeing her seated at one of the ancient, doodle-covered desks. I coasted all the way to lunch with nothing but a lot of curious looks, two more awkward public introductions, and a whole lot of sweat pouring down my neck and spine. No accusations of witchcraft yet. A small seedling of hope sprouted in my chest. Maybe I really would get to the end of the day unscathed. Maybe I hadn't messed up after all.

If only.

The cafeteria at this school was massive. I would have believed this room was a warehouse in its past life. Huge steel beams crisscrossed the ceiling, and the grimy, patchwork windows high above us let in just enough milky light to drape us in twilight instead of full darkness. It was like a weird industrial cathedral where we came to worship by eating over-salted and over-boiled food. Dozens upon dozens of round tables crowded the floor, most already full of students. While I still felt the weight of hundreds of wandering eyes searching for me, the crowd was moving so much that I could lose myself in the current weaving toward the buffet counters.

A hand clamped down on my shoulder and all but yanked me from the stream. The cold plastic of a chair pressed against the backs of my legs and I fell into it. I was at a mostly empty table at the edge of the cafeteria.

The table's only other occupant was that monstrous boy.

"We didn't get to finish our conversation from this morning," he said, leaning back in his chair like he was conducting a business meeting. Something about his demeanor had changed…his grossly entitled curiosity was replaced with menacing confidence. He was a cat playing with its catch, knowing that as soon as he decided to he could sink his claws into me. My hands curled into the fabric of my pants. I wanted nothing more than to show him exactly what he was toying with.

"I need to go—"

"You know, I heard the wildest thing about you. My girlfriend said…hang on, she should totally meet you." He turned toward the line of students forming around the food. "Caroline! Babe! Over here!"

His voice boomed across the cafeteria like a foghorn, and a girl with a perfectly coiffed blonde ponytail emerged from the mass of students. I recognized her from my first class. She had been sitting in the front row, eyes narrowed at me as I stumbled through my introduction. She beamed at the boy and headed over.

"She was saying that you moved here from a little town, right?"

A frigid spear pierced my stomach. I'd been expecting this from the girl I knocked over this morning, not from him. Had he felt the shock of magic earlier too somehow? That could explain the stench of smugness on him.

"Anyways, my cousin lives in a town a few hours' drive north. He was saying that a few weeks ago some weird girl at his school…"

His face went slack. Not just the spacing out kind of slack where your eyes unfocus and your mind is elsewhere, but the slack where the muscles in your mouth let go and drool leaks down your lip. His eyes, which were a murky hazel color, went flat, pupil-less gray like metal discs. He remained upright but hunched, like a powered-down robot.

No, no, nonono. This wasn't the turn I expected the day to take. Caroline was almost to the table and the room was filling with people and I didn't have time to figure out what kind of magic I did on this boy. I was out of control. I had to get out of this school now.

I stood and met the eyes of the last person I needed right now. Her cold, blue stare struck me like an arrow. The girl from this morning was on the opposite side of the cafeteria, hovering near an emergency exit and looking like an animal confronting oncoming headlights for the first time. Even at this distance I saw the tremor in her hands. A sheen of sweat covered her pale brow like dew. Frozen in that moment, her pallor grayed. Seeing me move, she bolted through the emergency exit. Bright light erased her silhouette as the door closed behind her.

Thought and action disconnected in my body. I knew that Caroline would arrive in seconds and see that her boyfriend was broken, and I knew that the girl with blue eyes was going to the authorities right now. I knew that I had to make this right for me and for my mom and for our future, whatever the cost. My feet were in motion before I decided what I could do.

A low, pained groan rose above the clamor behind me.

"Ugh…what happened?"

He was awake again. If the WRA didn't kill me by the end of the day, the adrenaline whiplash probably would.

I probably drew way more attention to myself than was smart as I threw myself out the emergency exit, but with each second that girl drew closer to condemning my mother to death.

The diffused light of the overcast day burned as the world oriented around me. I was in a loading dock area where trucks must drop off our government issued frozen lunches. Eight-foot-tall chain-link fences held back the tall buildings surrounding the school. This sad little courtyard was just as claustrophobic as the cafeteria. A rusty dumpster reeked against the fence, and a beautiful splash of neon graffiti across its front made it almost bearable to look at.

She sat against the wall of the loading dock, knees pulled up to her chest and head buried in her hands. She looked like a little doll, dwarfed by the buildings and the fence and the weight of the city hanging over us both. This wasn't the posture of someone running to the WRA…this was someone crying.

At the click of the door she leapt to her feet and raised her hands. Her cheeks were streaked with tear stains and her expression filled with familiar panic. The same panic I'd been swallowing since my bus ride this morning. Recognition bloomed under her fear, but her tension didn't ease.

"It's you," she said.

I had expected her voice to be breathy, wispy-sounding, but it was much deeper and richer than mine. It resonated in the base of my chest the way the low notes at the bottom of the old piano in our cottage used to.

"Mira, right?" she said.

"Uh…yeah."

I'd been vibrating with adrenaline for hours and guilty anxiety for weeks, but her voice made me still. Once, my mom took me to see the sequoia trees on the west coast and all I could think about as I stared up at their impossible heights was how deep their roots must go. Sequoia roots held me here, now, looking at her.

"I'm Sylvia."

Her name sounded like moonlight.

"Why—"

I wasn't able to ask the first of dozens of questions swirling around my head before the door behind me slammed open and Caroline stormed outside.

"*Witch!*" she snarled.

The word I'd been waiting to hear all day ricocheted against the concrete of the courtyard and inside my head like a silver bullet. All the *what ifs* I'd been entertaining evaporated as a metallic, dark taste settled in the back of my throat.

It was happening again.

I turned to face her, expecting to be met with bared teeth and clawed hands, but she brushed right by me. She brandished one of her manicured fingers at Sylvia like a dagger and didn't stop until she stood inches from her. Sylvia backed against the loading dock, looking so petrified she might disintegrate. Caroline towered over her.

"You enchanted Richie, you bitch, admit it. I saw you. He can't remember anything from the past month thanks to you and your disease. Admit it!"

Sylvia?

"I don't know what you're talking about," Sylvia said. Her voice shook like a dying leaf in an autumn storm. "Please, I don't—"

"Shut up. I saw you raise your hand at him and then he didn't remember anything. Admit it and I might only go to the police."

I held my breath as Sylvia raised a shaking hand to Caroline. New tears ran down her face, but magical energy hummed in the air as she grasped for some desperate lifeline inside her.

There was no doubting she was a witch.

"Don't you dare." Caroline snatched Sylvia's wrist and slammed it against the wall.

Sylvia's cry bounced off the courtyard, and something I couldn't name twinged in my chest.

"Did you really think I'd let you poison me too, freak?"

I felt like I was watching the day as an old VHS tape playing in reverse. This morning, Sylvia must have thought *she* was the one that did magic at *me*. I imagined her hiding around corners as I shuffled from class to class, believing that I was about to out her at my first chance.

But the boy. He knew. He said he heard a rumor about me. He was exuding smugness at having caught me in the lie until he just…stopped. And there was Sylvia, face pale and stricken. Whatever kind of enchantment she did saved me. She saved me in a room bursting with people who could have seen. And now she was pinned to jagged concrete, folded in defeat as Caroline demanded a confession.

She risked everything.

The school building stood behind me, an undeniably tempting escape. She made her choice fully knowing the risks. I couldn't be responsible for that when my mother was sitting at home, losing more color and life by the day. She'd already risked everything and lost it. For me.

I cracked open the cafeteria door to the sound of distant laughter, and a long-forgotten memory floated up from my subconscious. Me, sitting at home, watching through the window as kids from my elementary school walked home together. I heard them laughing as they prepared for a barbecue and a sleepover.

"You know why you can't be with them," Mom said. Sadness laced her voice. "I wish it didn't have to be like this."

It didn't have to be.

Loneliness strangled me every day I went back to a stagnant house with a mother who had nothing left. I made that flower bloom in the schoolyard back home because I thought I could find a cure for it somewhere else. But I'd been looking in the wrong place.

I never considered myself physically strong, but when I clamped down on Caroline's shoulders to yank her away from Sylvia she felt as light as a dandelion seed. We spun so that I stood between her and Sylvia. Utter, aghast rage twisted her expression.

"What the hell is *this?*"

"A warning."

I reached out to the pool of magic in my core and it answered like a stampede. Green, curling vines of energy thundered through my body and beyond. Weeds sprang up between the cracks in the concrete at my feet. I smiled in greeting at these living things I'd missed so much.

Caroline swiped for my face with her nails, but it was easy to duck out of the way. The air itself was pressing me on, willing me to win. She let out a wordless growl as she lunged for me again.

Bigger, I urged, and the weeds raced to obey. Thorny stems and bladed leaves grasped at Caroline's pristine designer sneakers and tangled in the hem of her leggings as they reached up her body.

"You're disgusting," she screeched. She scrabbled at the weeds, ripping them from the ground as fast as she could. I was faster. For each stem she snapped, another one twisted up her calves. Once they reached her knees, her frantic tearing turned desperate. I willed them to grow faster and they surged up her body, encasing her in a verdant embrace.

"Stop it." The steadfast righteousness she'd been threatening Sylvia with melted into a pathetic whimper.

"No."

The weeds climbed and climbed, thickening into solid, woody vines. Tears streaked her mascara as she pleaded with me to let her go, but I knew I had crossed a line and I had to see this through. And, if I was being honest with myself, it felt really good. In Caroline's place I saw Richie's face disappearing into the cocoon of vines, and then the man from the bus, and then every other stranger that looked at me with their hungry, possessive, mistrustful eyes. I wanted to work these disused parts of me for just a moment longer.

The vines stilled just short of her head. A leaf with a serrated edge settled just above Caroline's collarbone, not up against her neck but close enough to make her strain to get as far away from it as she could.

"Wh-what do you want?" she gasped.

"You're going to leave Sylvia alone and you're going to forget this ever happened," I said. I surprised myself with how steady I sounded with the power raging inside me. I hadn't ever let this much magic channel through me, and the rush of euphoria that followed it was breathtaking.

"Mira."

Sylvia's hand closed around mine and that same jolt of pure, white energy sang through my body again. Only this time, I was already bursting with magic, and she wasn't letting go.

We must have burned like the sun in that courtyard.

The air around us lost its musty, trash smell and grew sweet with the smell of fresh herbs and sun-soaked earth. The light in the courtyard took on a golden sheen and warmth impossible to find in October. It was like standing in a garden. *My* garden. We were still surrounded by skyscrapers and rusty fences, but the air that moved through this space now smelled of leaves and dirt and the first magnolias of summer.

"You can smell that?" I whispered.

"Of course I can," Sylvia said.

Caroline let out a nasally sob. "Please let me go."

Sylvia reached around me with her free hand and held it over Caroline's face. "Forget."

Caroline's eyes blinked to that same flat gray that the boy's eyes had been. Her body slumped, and if it weren't for my plants she probably would have collapsed to the ground.

"How are you doing it?" Sylvia asked. "I've never seen magic like this before."

"I have a plant affinity, but there's no way I could do something like this—the smell, the light." I breathed in the scent of home, almost expecting the herb beds and rickety stone wall of the garden to appear around us.

"I do memories," she said.

"Then this has to be you." I gestured to the air around us. "It's one of my memories."

"I can't do that. I can barely do what I did to Richie and Caroline."

"Then it's got to be both of us. Together."

"I've never heard of witches being able to affect each other's magic."

I frowned. "Me neither. But I guess…I don't really know much about magic."

"Me neither."

Sylvia squeezed my wrist then let her hand drop. The smell faded and the air stilled. I wanted to suck up every last hint of home and bottle it forever, but it slipped away too fast. I met Sylvia's gaze and the atmosphere around us thrummed with something obvious and old.

A truck blared out on the street and pulled me back into the reality of standing in a loading dock behind the school with a comatose classmate wrapped in vines. I shook from the intensity of the last minute, and Sylvia trembled. Her pale cheeks flushed and she looked away. My own face warmed.

Had that really just happened?

"Come on," she said. "We need to get her back."

"She really won't remember this?"

"I don't think so…but there's no guarantee."

There couldn't be, not after this. I released one last pulse of magic and the weeds uncurled from Caroline's body and retreated back beneath the concrete. Sylvia waved a hand in front of her face again and Caroline mechanically marched back inside.

"She'll be fine in a moment." Sylvia let out a huff of air and began to follow Caroline, but stopped. "Mira?"

"Yeah?"

"Could we…could we do it again sometime? Whatever this was?"

I had to bite back the enthusiastic *yes* that so badly wanted to burst out of me. I imagined my mom, standing in the doorway of our apartment, bags under her eyes and all the magic gone from the air around her. I saw her looking with horror as Sylvia and I made joyful ribbons of magic soar around the kitchen. I felt the disappointment, fear, and rage radiating off of her, same as the night we had to flee from our last home. I pictured her shoving Sylvia out the door, ensuring we were safely alone together again, the colorless walls of our normal apartment bearing down on us forever.

We're not witches here.

Sylvia's eyes were the color of spring's first bluebells, and when the *yes* fell from my lips I felt like I was standing in a field full of them, a warm breeze twirling around me and pulling me forward, away from gray walls and suffocating air.

"Yes," I repeated, and let the promise of magic wrap around us with color and sound, carrying all the promise of summer and laughter and *togetherness* with it. We existed here. We twisted magic around us like glittering scarves and danced under the warmth of the sun. We were witches, and we burned with light.

What's Easier

by
Nathan Moone

Jules didn't mind the taste of dirt on his lips. When he leaned forward to kiss Ray's cheek, his best friend froze. Pale white light illuminated the tent just enough for the two boys to see each other.

"What?" Jules said as his heart thundered.

"Boys don't do that with each other."

"But we did."

"I guess so."

Crickets covered the drumming of their heartbeats. Leaves quietly fell to the wind. The cool air of fall made the tent feel cramped while they both bundled under their layers of blankets.

Ray turned away to lay down in the sleeping bag.

"Was that okay?" Jules stared at the dark shape in the bag next to him.

"Yeah."

They were still. Jules laid his head down and attempted to push the image of his father out of his mind. Every day for the last couple weeks his father brought up the move while wearing the widest smile. How could he be so happy to leave everything behind?

Jules still remembered the smell of burnt rubber from the skid marks he and Ray created a few summers back when they rode home from the park on their bikes. How could he be so happy to leave behind family? How could he expect Jules to leave his best friend?

"Jules?"

"Yeah?"

Ray's silence was too heavy to break. In the end, Jules couldn't say goodbye; it was easier to kiss him instead.

***

It was near impossible to walk through the lunchroom without bumping into someone else. Jules held his lunch box close while he walked past crowded tables. No one seemed to be bothered by the incessant shouting of annoying teenagers. Every available seat screamed *avoid me!* Lunch had never been this obnoxious before. Jules searched as best he could to find any familiar faces from his childhood. No one stood out despite there being a hundred or so students crammed into the room. Nobody looked how they did in elementary school. After a week of being here, he hoped to have recognized someone by now. Then again, he had only eaten in the lunchroom once since starting the new school year. High school wasn't as inviting as he had hoped, more so because he missed the first week of school and transferred in on the second.

With each lap around the room, more students crowded in. As Jules reached the front yet again, he looked to see if any teachers were paying attention. All of them were too busy scanning the back of the room for any trouble to notice Jules slip out of the lunchroom and head to the library. Better than eating in a hallway. At least the library was quieter and had chairs with cushions on them.

The librarian at the front counter gave Jules a sweet smile and nod. He was beginning to look forward to seeing Mrs. Dior at lunch, an older woman who'd been nothing but kind. She always brought a worry-free feeling to the room, which made it all the better when Jules was able to find a comfortable area in the corner of the library. Across from him was another small group of students, all oddballs of the school. A little rambunctious, but overall not a concern. They spoke loud enough to keep Jules entertained while he zipped open his lunch box to start nibbling on his food. He couldn't take more than a few bites.

By the end of seventh period, Jules was more than ready to go home and bury himself in his bed. He did his best to keep as calm as he could in last period, but Mr. Vargas had a fondness for big group activities. Today, Mr. Vargas had everyone stand up and then asked a question. The left side of the room was answer A, the right was answer B. While Jules was deciding whether to go to the left or right side of the room for the question, he blanked out until his teacher said, "Thank you again, Ray!"

Ray? Jules nearly frightened the girl next to him at the sudden snap of his head as he tried to get a good look at who this "Ray" was. He handed Mr. Vargas a small food container and left the room in a few short strides. This gave Jules plenty of time to stare in shock as Ray shut the door behind him.

"Ummm, you good?" the girl to Jules' left asked.

When he looked over at her she leaned back.

"You're not gonna puke, are you?" she asked louder.

"What? No! I'm not gonna—" Jules lowered his voice when he realized others were looking at him. "No, I'm not going to throw up. Just thought I saw something."

She rolled her eyes and looked away.

Jules did his best to ignore her and tried to breathe. Was that really the same boy who had been his childhood best friend? Ray looked harder now than he did at eleven. The scowl on his face was more than enough to deter anyone from approaching him. The dark fuzz of early facial hair covered his lip and chin. Jules began to think back to the night in the tent.

"What side are you choosing, Jules?" The brass voice of Mr. Vargas broke his trance.

On opposite ends of the classroom the rest of the class watched.

"I'm sorry, I'll move to this side," Jules said. He could practically feel his insides shrinking in on themselves.

Mr. Vargas hushed the snickers. The right side of the room watched Jules approach. The room grew hotter with each step. He made himself comfortable in the back of the group, wanting nothing more than to phase out of existence. Everyone else seemed to enjoy being up and moving around; the other students took advantage of the coordinated chaos to talk to and annoy one another. Jules couldn't recall most of their names just yet.

"Excuse me," said a girl to his left.

He did his best to avoid fidgeting with his hands at the thought of this new human contact.

"Can you move over a bit please? I wanna talk to Julia."

Julia didn't wait for him to move as she wedged herself into Jules' space.

Jules took a step back, keeping his deep exhale as quiet as he could.

"Now," Mr. Vargas announced, "how many of you—"

A shrill bell cut him off to signal the end of the day. All the students rushed back to their assigned seats to collect their stuff. Jules stayed put on the side of the room while he waited for his row to clear out. Everyone poured out of the room within moments. Even after a week of being in school, he couldn't believe the feral energy of these kids. This could not at all compare to how his last school operated. Jules walked to his desk and bent over to pick up his brand-name backpack. He hated it. No one else had a giant bright white logo on their bag. The other kids probably picked out their own bags. As if he wasn't standing out already as the new kid from NYC. Jules slung his bag over his shoulder and walked out of the class, keeping an eye out for a familiar face.

Jules had yet to get his locker open on the first try, never mind trying to find someone who may as well be a stranger. Someone who could have left school already. Jules had to fight for each breath, his chest feeling tighter with each passing moment. Not like the confusing layout of the school helped keep his heart from beating out of his chest. By the time Jules reached his locker, his ride home, bus 12, would already be long gone.

On his third attempt at fiddling with his lock, the blue metal of his locker door clicked open. It was bare on the inside, unlike most of the lockers he'd seen. Jules fidgeted with the contents of his bag, exchanging his math and science books for the lunch box that was still practically full.

Down the hall, a conversation grew nearer as Jules pulled his wireless earbuds from his bag. He pressed both buds in and turned the corner to make for the exit to the anthem of Fall Out Boy. Two students hung posters for something called GSA as he passed. He couldn't hear them clearly over the sound of Patrick Stump's vibrato, but recognition struck him as the two turned the corner and walked out of sight.

Once his brain stopped flailing for what to do, Jules took out his earbuds and shoved them in their case as he jogged back to his locker. Just a few lockers away, Ray and some girl were pushing each other playfully, arms stacked with colorful posters. Despite both of their backs facing him, Jules recognized the girl from the library when he'd eat there. Their laughter rang out in the empty hall as they jabbed at each other.

He has a girlfriend. *That's...great.* Jules couldn't force himself to catch up with them just yet. Instead, he stayed behind to observe. How long had that been going on for? A bout of annoyance wormed its way into him. How much could he have changed? It had been four years; of course he had a new best friend.

Ray hung another poster as they spoke. Jules was close enough to hear them, but did his best not to eavesdrop, obviously. He got nervous when he thought Ray looked his way.

"Why you can't just admit season six is better than five is beyond me." Ray's voice was clear in the hall.

"Six!? Oh please!" the girl from the library snapped. "Five is so much better than six! Six was good, but by far five was the best thing that could have happened for RuPaul, periodt!"

"Whatever you say hunty, all I can hear is denial."

"Bah, to hell with you. Let me get the last of the flyers from the library and we can finish up the lunchroom, 'kay?" she said and skipped down the hall.

Ray waved to her back and called, "I'll grab the cutouts from my locker!"

Jules closed the distance between himself and Ray as he followed him to his locker. What if he didn't remember him? No one seemed to remember Jules in the four years that he'd been gone. At lunch last week his former teammate, Brian, stared blankly at him when Jules asked if he could sit with him and his football squad. Would Ray be any different?

Ray and his flashy hand-patched jacket stood out against the soulless blue paint of the lockers as he walked. Ray worked on his lock and flung the door open with ease.

Just go up to him. Pull it off like a Band-Aid.

Ray pulled a wad of decorations from his locker.

Jules raised an eyebrow. Rainbows?

Ray shut his locker and flicked through the colorful papers as he walked. He flicked his gaze up at Jules when he neared, then his gaze went back down to the papers. Jules didn't dare to even blink as Ray walked past. Ray's dark converse squeaked sharply against the tiles as he stopped short. Ray slowly turned around to meet Jules' eyes.

"Hi, Ray." For all the time he spent thinking about what to say, Jules couldn't get further than that.

"Jules?" Ray crossed to his side of the hall. "Wow, I didn't even recognize you. Didn't expect to see you here," he said.

"Yeah, my family and I just moved back recently." Jules put his all into sounding more confident than he felt.

"Nice."

An uneasy silence followed. It was shocking how loud the silence seemed as they both scanned the hallway as if admiring the scenery.

"Sooo," Ray said, "how was the Big Apple?"

"It was nice!" Jules' voice echoed in the hallway, and Ray cringed at the volume.

"It was good. Got to walk the city every day," he said quieter. "Saw some cool celebrities, you know, all that fun stuff. Added to my collection of Pokémon cards since I last saw you. I'll have to show you sometime."

"I got rid of mine a while ago. But that's cool." Ray fiddled with the rainbows in his hands. "Listen, I have to get going. I have to hang up some decorations for my group. We could catch up sometime?"

His opportunity was slipping through his fingers. "Ah that's fine, I get it. What club are you a part of? Maybe I can help out." He forced a laugh.

"The GSA."

"Oh cool! I was actually going to check that out myself." His forehead tingled with droplets of sweat. He didn't even know what the GSA was.

"Okay. Uh, sure, I guess that would be alright. Skye and I will appreciate it." Ray rubbed at the back of his neck. A glint of silver flashed from his right ear.

The heat returned to his face at the mention of the girl.

"Thanks! I missed my bus already, so I don't have anywhere else to be." Jules quickly added, "is Skye your…girlfriend?"

Ray looked down at the rainbows in his hands and back up to Jules. "You certainly are new here, aren't you?"

"I mean yeah, that's why I want to get involved with something."

"Never learned to lie even after all this time." He turned around and headed down the hall.

"Wait! Hold on. I didn't mean anything by asking—" He didn't finish, opting to run after Ray instead.

"Do you even know what it means?"

"What, GSA?"

"Yeah." Ray turned with a flat look on his face.

"Of course…not." They reached the short staircase leading to the lunchroom, and Ray stopped and leaned against the wall. This corner of the school was empty now that the buses had left.

"We are the Gender and Sexuality Alliance. We are open to whoever wants to join, queer kids and allies alike. But if you don't actually want to be there then you won't be a good fit." Ray crossed his arms.

Jules wanted to sink into the floor. It felt like the time his mom said she "wasn't mad, just disappointed."

"Wait so you're…queer?" He caught himself from saying gay.

"Oh boy, on that note…" Ray started down the steps.

"It's totally okay if you are!" He bounded after him. "I'm taking in a lot right now. I'm sorry."

"Then thanks for your permission."

"No, I didn't mean—shit." Jules stopped at the bottom of the stairs.

Ray kept on moving.

"I am being far from a friend right now and I realize that was rude to say and to ask of you."

Ray moved on and disappeared around the corner. His steps echoed in the emptiness of the school.

"But I was really hoping that we could be friends again. I even missed my bus trying to talk to you!" Jules jogged to catch up to him.

Ray stopped to face Jules. "I'd appreciate the help you're offering, and I'd like to think that four years of being gone hasn't turned you into a homophobe." He handed Jules a stack of decorations. "So please, for the love of God, please try and learn something."

Jules thought it was best to respond with a short and simple nod.

"And if that didn't answer your question, no. Skye and I aren't dating," Ray said. "Now, how about you help me set up the group's spot for the bake sale this week."

A familiar voice called out behind them. "Are you sure you wouldn't rather be asking me out instead Ray? I'm sure my dad would love that."

"Well, then I'm happy to disappoint!" Ray said, a warm smile replacing his neutral expression.

Jules turned around to see Skye walking towards them. Now that he could see her face, the first thing that he noticed was the giant rubber ducks that dangled from her earrings. The front of her tie-dyed shirt had bright white text that read "Kiss Whoever the F#ck You Want."

"I see you made a friend." She gestured at Jules with the stack of flyers in her hand.

"You could say that. This is Jules. He and I were friends when we were younger. He just moved back from NYC," Ray said.

"Jules? Why does that sound familiar? He moved right before we met in middle school, right?"

"That's the one."

"I can imagine you two have a lot to catch up on." Skye looked down at the rainbows in the boys' hands. "Good thing your best friend is around to help fill in the dots." A quiet moment passed between her and Ray before she smiled. "It's nice to meet you."

"Thanks, you too," Jules said. "I recognize you from the library. You sit in the back with your friends near the windows during lunch sometimes."

"As much as we can honestly, can't even hear whoever is sitting across from me half the time in the caf." She tilted her head. "Do you usually sit with Martin and his group?"

"Nah. I don't really have a group to sit with just yet." He didn't want to explain that he also sat near the windows often, on the couches no more than two tables over from where her group usually sat.

"Help us set this up and maybe you'll have a group to sit with tomorrow." A smile curved her lips. "Though if you're friends with Ray, I'm sure that won't be a problem anymore. He makes sure all of us gaybies are taken care of."

"Gaybies?"

Skye set her flyers down on the table next to her. "You know, his gay babies. You didn't hear that in NYC?"

"I went to an all-boys Catholic school. Being gay wasn't really a thing there," Jules admitted.

"Oh, you'd be surprised," Ray said.

"Plus, that was middle school. All this stuff happens in high school anyway," Jules said. "Or so I've heard."

Ray's eyes widened at that. He and Skye shared a look with one another.

"Wait," Skye said, "wasn't he your first kiss or something? Is he even—"

"How about Jules and I take it from here? I would like to catch up with J one-on-one if you don't mind."

Jules' insides felt like molten lava as he watched Skye raise her hands in defeat.

"Alright sheesh, I'll leave you two alone." She backed away. "Text me later tonight so I can make sure you're…okay."

"Will do." Ray shot her a peace sign as she turned the corner and left the lunchroom. "I'm sorry about her. That wasn't right of her to bring any of that up or to ask you that question. I'll tell her later that wasn't cool."

"It's fine. She has every right to be suspicious. I'll be okay. She is your best friend after all." He cleared his throat and turned to look down at the flyers. "How should I go about putting these up? Just let me know what to do."

Ray pursed his lips and took a deep breath. "Just follow my lead and we will be out of here in twenty." Ray moved away and redoubled his efforts on the posters. "But later we are going to continue this conversation."

Jules nodded and blinked away the moisture in his eyes.

Is he even— Skye's question rang in his head. His answer was noticeably absent.

***

59

Once the last flier was taped to the wall, the front of the lunchroom had a bit more pizazz than when they first started. Various printouts of pride flags hung on the wall, and the table they'd be using had a bright, colorful banner displaying SUPPORT YOUR GSA in bold letters along with a smaller PRIDE CUPCAKES—$5.

"This is gonna go fantastic tomorrow. Thanks for helping us out, Jules." Ray beamed, admiring their handiwork. "Now if you don't mind, I'd love to get out of here."

"It's the least I can do. I didn't know there was stuff like this in high school."

"I'm surprised." Ray picked up the pace as they left the lunchroom and started towards the exit.

"Why's that?"

"Ever since you left, I've kinda been curious about how you turned out. I mean, not to be too bold or anything, but seeing as you were the one who kissed me when we were twelve, I figured you'd be well on your way down this path already. Especially in New York."

A weight formed in his stomach. "It was only on the cheek. And besides, there isn't much queer culture in my house."

"That's what started all this for me," Ray said nonchalantly, adjusting the straps of his backpack as they crossed the main foyer.

It took a moment to adjust to the bright autumn sunlight pouring in from the windows. Ray pushed the exit door open and Jules walked out behind him.

Jules waited until the door closed firmly behind them with a loud click. "What do you mean by 'all this?'"

"Me being queer. Is it that much of a surprise?"

"I mean. Kind of. Not like I've been able to keep tabs on you." A long black fence guided the boys on their right as they left school property. Jules took long strides while they went down what he knew as the "death hill." Always busy with cars or buses, with a four-way intersection moderated by a constantly broken traffic light. Today there wasn't a human soul in sight. Birds skittered across the empty roads, pecking at anything that might be food, Band-Aids and worms included. Splashes of color spotted the street as fading leaves fell from their trees.

"Where's home for you? I only live a short walk away," Ray said.

"About a fifteen-minute drive away on Drawbridge. Did you move?" Jules asked.

"After my parents split, mom and I had to. We're only a few streets away from school now. So, it worked out."

"Oh, I'm sorry. I didn't know that."

"How could you? It's fine." A single bike whipped by and kicked up a rush of yellow and orange leaves.

"Seems like you've been busy over the last few years." Jules meant it as a joke to lighten the mood, but regretted it after hearing how it came out.

"Kind of a domino effect, really. My best friend leaves at twelve, I come out as gay at fourteen, parents split at fifteen, disowned by dad also at fifteen." Ray's voice was shockingly calm and factual.

How could he be okay after going through all of that? Jules did his best to squash down all of the questions that came to mind, but guilt pinched at his neck for speculating about what Ray must have gone through after he left. Each step felt heavier next to Ray as they walked. Did he even have the right to feel horrible about it? Jules gathered enough courage to say, "I feel like I should apologize…"

"None of it was your fault," he said. "Maybe except the gay thing."

"I see."

"I guess by that knowledge then, this would all be your fault."

Jules tensed until Ray smirked at him.

"Asshole."

"Though how about you? Must not have been all sunshine and rainbows."

A line of cars drove by them as they walked down the sidewalk and the wind buffeted their clothes.

"Everything had been quiet until recently really," Jules admitted. "Dad got fired from the job that moved us in the first place, so we decided to come back to Rhode Island. My mom and dad are always working so I have a lot of free time." He undid the top few buttons on his light blue button-up.

"Feel free to attend a GSA meeting if you feel up to it. Though I'm sure there are other clubs you'd be more interested in," Ray said.

"Why do you think that?"

"You said it yourself, you're only interested in it because I'm a part of it."

"Well yeah, but I liked what I saw today. The group seems pretty cool. Plus, it would probably be good to actually educate myself on this stuff. Who knows, maybe I'm gay and don't know it yet."

"Yes, I'm sure you and your khaki pants and button-ups will soon be accompanied by a rainbow flag cape and RuPaul mannerisms." Ray rolled his eyes.

"From what I've seen on Twitter, being queer comes in all shapes and sizes, so what if button-ups and khakis are one of them?"

Ray's face scrunched like he was contemplating the question. "My house is just a few blocks away. We can sit in my room until Mom comes home."

Jules nodded and let Ray lead the way.

***

The house Ray led him to was not at all like he imagined. Ray used to live in a pretty sweet two-story house with a huge backyard to play football in, but sitting in front of him was a plain, light blue duplex. Behind the fence, a rusty swing set creaked in the light wind with a deflated pool beside it. Jules almost invited him to his place to check out his in-ground pool, but choked off the words and stayed silent. Would Ray still be helping him make friends if he saw what his house looked like?

"Mom should be back in a little bit. I'm sure she could drive you home if you'd like." Ray left the door open for Jules to follow.

Lavender gently scented the air as he entered the living room. The same light brown leather couch he spilled Kool-Aid on one summer sat in a corner. He'd been too nervous to tell Ray's parents he'd spilled the drink, and the dark stain still showed on the arm. Despite the new layout, he recognized most of their furniture. It looked like Ray's dad took his sports memorabilia. The few new photos on display showed Ray in a different style: less punky and more domestic. He paused on a particular photo. One with Ray and him posing for the camera in front of an old Navy ship that visited Newport years ago.

Ray stomping up the stairs pulled Jules from his thoughts. He walked up the tight stairway lit by a bare yellow bulb. Jules resisted the impulse to swipe at the dangling string hanging from it. A black Fall Out Boy poster covered the wooden door on the left side of the hall. When Ray opened the door, the distinct smell of boy caught up to Jules, a mix of feet and Doritos. Vastly different from his own room, which had a scent-boosting, beach-themed plug-in his mom put there.

The room wasn't messy, but it was not clean—organized chaos that only a growing teen could make.

"Not quite like what you remember, huh?"

His room was much smaller than the one they used to hang out in. He had enough room for his twin bed to sit in the far corner, his flat-screen across from it, and a dresser. Posters and pictures covered the majority of the four walls. A rainbow flag with a coffee-like stain on the bottom portion hung over his bed.

"Less Pokémon and Dragon Ball than I remember, if that's what you mean."

Ray dropped his bag by the foot of his bed and fell flat onto his back, bouncing twice before the springs settled. A deep exhale lowered his chest. Jules also dropped his bag and turned away from Ray to examine the rest of his room.

"Mom's usually home by 4:30, so she should be home in less than an hour," Ray said to the ceiling.

"Thanks. I'm gonna tell my parents that I stayed after to help you out with a project."

"Don't feel comfortable telling them about the GSA?" Ray asked.

"I don't know if I want to commit to the line of questioning that will come with that."

Ray didn't move for a bit, simply lay down on the bed without a sound other than his breathing.

"Thanks for letting me tag along." Jules didn't have anything else to look at, so he sat on the wooden floor.

"It's been cool seeing you again. A bit strange though."

"We've both changed a little."

"A little?" Ray sat up and pointed at Jules. "Boy, you're white bread and I'm sourdough."

"Pardon me for wanting to look good." Jules laughed.

"Pardon me? My, don't you sound sophisticated."

Jules was painfully aware of the differences between the two of them but did his best to play it off. "I can rip off my sleeves and dye my hair black if that's better. I can be edgy if I want." Most notably, if he did that his parents would absolutely ground him. Ray didn't seem like he'd be deterred by mere threats or groundings. If anything, from the few fucks he'd given so far, he'd probably be spurred on.

"Now that I'd pay to see."

"I think my dad would flip if I came home with dyed hair."

"Just wait until you're dating." Ray sat up. "I can bet no one would be good enough for dad's golden boy." Ray smiled.

Jules didn't quite know how to respond to that. His smile faded, but it's not like he could be too offended by that. Why did he even feel offended in the first place?

"How did you know you were, you know, gay?" Jules finally asked.

"Oh God, here we go—"

"What? This is my first time learning about queer stuff, I think that gets a pass," he countered.

"Oh God, you're lucky I'm trying to make you a good ally." Ray kicked his shoes off. "It started in middle school when I noticed I wasn't having crush after crush like the other boys. When I thought about kissing or anything related to it, I always thought back to you. Kind of hard to move past your first experience. Even harder when the girls I did kiss didn't give me a 'floaty' feeling."

Jules' mouth went dry. What Ray described was familiar. It scared him as much as it relieved the tension in his stomach.

"The internet came in to save me from going down that rabbit hole alone," Ray continued. "So a few Google searches later, I came across the LGBT community and that was that."

Jules waited for him to continue. Ray didn't.

"That was that? It just, poof, happened that easy?" Jules said louder than he meant.

"Finding out you're gay and applying it to your life are two totally separate battles," Ray said. "Finding out won't have consequences. Actually living as a gay guy does."

"What are the consequences?" Jules asked.

"They change every day."

"That's a little…dramatic."

"I'm gay, of course I'm dramatic." He laughed lightly. "Doesn't mean it's any less true though. I'm sure you get at least a little bit of it from yourself. That voice in your head telling you that something about you is off. It's not like every boy that sees their old best friend secretly follows them in the halls."

Heat rose in Jules' cheeks. "You knew I was following you?"

"I didn't know it was you, I just figured you were another kid looking to use me as an experiment for their sexuality. That's how it always starts, some rando follows you around and tries to kiss or date you in secret to get a feel for what's confusing them."

"You say this like it's happened before."

"We're in high school, this sort of thing happens all the time." Ray stood up from his bed and tidied his dresser.

"People harassing you?"

"That's not how they see it." Ray picked up the empty soda cans from the floor and tossed them into the small trash can next to the dresser. "Puberty is happening and no one is being educated on sex, let alone sexuality. Of course teens are going to take it into their own hands. A majority of them just don't think about how it can hurt others."

Jules looked down to the floor.

"So, what's a little kiss with the out kid in your school, or a little more than that? If you don't like it, you can just deny it."

"I'm sorry for having you think that's who I was at first. I didn't know how to approach you," Jules said.

"You could have just said hi. Once I realized you weren't one of those kids, I figured you wanted to try and start shit or something. Then your face clicked."

"I tried that at lunch with Brian and he looked at me like I had four heads."

"With the number of concussions he's had I'm sure that's how you looked."

His joking burned Jules' patience faster.

"I was at least hoping one person would recognize me. Being back in a public school has already been stressful enough, but high school too? I'm already starting late into the year, so I feel excluded enough." Jules took a deep breath to steady his nerves. "You're also like, the first person I've even been able to talk to about this."

"Feel free to let it out if you want, it's not like I'm going anywhere." Ray shrugged.

"It's been hard coming back here after all these years. I don't know anyone, I feel so out of place, and the last thing I did with you was kiss you." Jules couldn't take sitting down anymore, so he stood up to pace the room. "Now for the first time I'm actually confronting a very real possibility that I'm not, as you said, 'white bread' and I don't know what to do about it!"

Jules didn't realize he was raising his voice until he stopped talking. He took a breath.

"I don't even know if I can call you my friend? I legit just followed you to a club and invited myself over to your place because I don't know anyone else."

Ray leaned against his desk, his eyes wide as he nodded. "To be fair, I offered to take you to my place because you were my friend. I can't say we're best friends anymore. But that doesn't mean that can't change."

"I only said all that 'cause you said to." Jules couldn't bring himself to make eye contact. He could only imagine how much Ray would be judging him. The private school daddy's boy who wants to be quirky and join the latest fad of being queer. He turned around to lose himself in the posters on the wall.

"It was quite…"

"Dramatic?" Jules asked.

"I was going to say depressing, but I can't say I can't relate."

Jules chuckled despite himself.

"I'm not gonna come out and say I have all the answers for you, I don't even know how to answer my own doubts. But I can tell you one day you'll have more answers." Ray reached for his hand.

Jules jumped at the unexpected contact but let Ray lead him to the bed to sit him down. "After you left, I didn't think there was anything good to come. After my parents divorced, I changed my mind about that. I can only say this now from a distance, but it'll be okay. This isn't just toxic positivity either. For you and me both."

"It's just…different," Jules said.

"How so?"

"I don't even know why this is happening. I get that I kissed you and that's what made you start questioning. But we were kids. I didn't kiss you because I wanted to like…" Jules lowered his voice, "be with you. It just sort of happened. You didn't even like it, if I remember right."

Ray squeezed Jules' hand tighter and took his time to respond. "Is that why you're so unsure? Because you think I didn't like it?"

"No," Jules said. "Well, maybe a bit. I just…don't know why I did it. It just happened. And knowing that I could have been the reason why you turned out gay just confuses me even more. I didn't have anything that made me start to question until I began to reflect on that night. Every single night I was away I kept thinking of how I may have ruined our friendship. Maybe that's why I never called. I don't know, man." Jules let go of Ray's hand and clutched at the loose fabric of his pants.

"I wish we knew then what we know now." Ray sighed. "Back then I was a little weirded out, don't get me wrong, but I knew it was because you cared. You may have kissed my cheek, but if you think that's what 'turned' me gay, then I'm gonna have to disappoint you there."

"But wasn't I—"

"Sweetie, that kiss isn't what defines your sexuality, or mine for the matter. This here, us talking, is what can give you answers that tearing yourself down can't provide. We've been talking what? Maybe a few hours and already you're understanding more. You're not going to have an answer tonight."

"I'm not expecting an answer tonight," Jules said.

"If you'd like, I can take you to our meeting next week?"

"Do my parents have to know?"

"No, they don't," Ray said. "Do you think they would do something if they found out?"

"No. I mean, maybe. It's never been brought up before."

"Either way, we can keep this to ourselves until you're ready. This is your journey."

"But what if I'm wrong? I mean, what if I am straight and I'm just, I don't know—"

"Curious? Confused?" Ray smiled at Jules.

Jules' racing thoughts slowed. Ray was good.

"My confusion is where I found myself. It's the scariest part by far, but with friends like Skye and me, maybe we can make these questions go by a bit easier." Ray stood from his bed and offered a hand to Jules. "At the very least I'm not gonna be having my friend eat alone at lunch. Now come on, it's been too long since I've played catch."

"Yeah," Jules said. "I'd like that a lot." He accepted the hand up.

***

Even after a full night's rest—the easiest sleep he'd had since coming back home—Jules still felt the giddiness from newfound freedom. Because both his mom and dad were out of the house before he could wake up, no one complained to him for rolling up the sleeves of his nice striped button-up. He smiled each time his unbuttoned shirt flapped open from a breeze and revealed the golden Pikachu shirt he bought from a store in the big city. His dad would have called it unprofessional, but Jules was sure Ray would think otherwise. He knew he made the right decision when a classmate actually complimented it before the first bell rang.

Classes went the same as they had been, though time seemed to be flying by. Up until lunch, at least. He spent so much time trying to commit to his outfit, he totally forgot to pack his own lunch. Every circular table was filled with a group of friends either laughing or talking with mouths full. Jules stood in line waiting for food, scanning the room for a spot to sit that wasn't the super long lunch table. All the loud kids sat there. He kept focusing on the spot where the GSA bake sale should be, but only printouts occupied the space. *Maybe they aren't selling for this lunch?*

"Next," the lunch lady said in monotone.

Jules stepped forward and input his lunch code, then grabbed a slice of a soggy-looking pizza and a bag of chips. He returned to the tables and stood still. The longer he waited, the more eyes he felt on him. Jules shook his head and wished he could phase through the lunchroom. He did his best to try and sneak all the way through and got as far as the steps before a teacher stopped him.

"Where are you off to? Food isn't allowed to leave the lunchroom," a woman with a dark ponytail said.

Jules faintly remembered seeing her teach in the history hall.

"I'm going to the library. I've always eaten there."

"Not today you're not. Let's try and make you some new friends, yeah?" she said, almost like he had a choice.

"I'd rather not."

"If that's—"

"Hello, Mrs. Langer!" Ray strode in carrying sealed trays of cupcakes, just in time to save the day. "Jules was meant to give us an extra hand, but we're all set now to head back. Ready, Jules?"

Mrs. Langer eyed them, and her eyebrow twitched before she answered. "Alright, boys. Then you best get back." She stared at Jules a second longer before walking off.

Ray gestured his head to follow.

"All good?" he asked.

"I was about to head to the library. Thought you weren't going to be at lunch this period." Jules followed Ray back to the caf.

"I thought I told you you weren't going to be eating alone at lunch anymore?"

"I didn't see you or Skye set up anywhere. Plus, it felt like everyone was just staring at me standing doing nothing so…"

"They were probably just staring at your dope-ass shirt," Ray said, placing the trays down at the decorated table at the front of the lunchroom.

Jules' cheeks flashed with the heat of invisible flames.

"A little less white bread I think."

"More whole-grain now." Ray stepped back to stand next to Jules and admire his handiwork. "I think it's about time to start."

"Okay, uh, where should I sit then?"

"Hmm? Oh, you can sit here with us." Ray gestured to the table. "If you're comfortable, that is. Shit, I didn't even think. I can introduce—"

"I'll sit here with you both, that's okay."

"Sweet, just please throw that so-called pizza out. Have a cupcake for God's sake, and I have extra food in my bag you can have," Ray told him.

"You're a lifesaver, you know that?"

"Rainbow package and all." Ray took the plate from Jules' hands and tossed it in the trash. "How about we get started, huh? Skye should be here any moment. Sound good?"

"Sounds perfect."

The Blue Jay Journal

by
Sarah DeCataldo

October 24, 2018

Dear Agnes,

Nicole gave me this journal today. She thought writing about my feelings could help me process that you're dying. I'm sure her psychology degree makes her qualified to offer the suggestion, but for me losing you is unimaginable. Regardless, our granddaughter certainly is thoughtful. I got bored just sitting here, so I figured I would give it a shot.

The news isn't good, Agnes. You're sedated, and the doctor doesn't expect you to wake up before it happens. I read to you, though. Your favorite—Agatha Christie. And I talk to you a lot too. The hospital chaplain, Father Brian, encouraged me to. He said you could hear me. I'm not sure if you can, but I keep on talking. For all I know, you may be telling me to shut up. Although, you only tell me to shut up when I'm talking during your *Real Housewives* shows. I don't understand how you can watch that smut. And those New Jersey ones make us Italians look bad. You call them your girls. Secretly, I enjoy the drama, but I know you already know that.

Father Brian comes up daily to pray with us. He's a young Irish kid. Red hair, freckles. Oh, and tall. You would call him a "tall drink of water." He is very kind. He has been spending a lot of time talking with me about you, about us. I've shared a lot with him: how we met, our first kiss in 1958, our friendship and love, and how we finally came out to our children and families. It felt good to talk about all we went through—the struggle of being in love but not being able to be with one another. And we talk about all of the things I am going to miss about you too. The way we snuggled at night and watched reruns of our favorite TV shows. The little things you did for us, like how you always made sure the coffee was made in the morning, how there was always a spare roll of toilet paper in the bathroom, and how you always hid one sleeve of Thin Mint cookies in the back of the freezer for emergencies.

Grief is a strange thing. It feels different with each person you lose. Losing my husband to cancer, I felt relief. Losing Robert, my only biological child, was numbing. But through all of those losses, all of that pain, you were beside me. Holding me while I cried, helping me not curl up and die myself. You always gave me hope. Who is going to help me get through the loss of you? I'm scared, Agnes. The thought of living life without you physically hurts. My chest gets heavy. My head starts spinning. I have to catch my breath. Being in this world without you is a pain I had never imagined. I know we had over sixty years together—forty-two as best friends and twenty as wives. Well, technically, only five years as wives legally, but you know how we both feel about that—goddamned politician crooks.

Anyway, I want sixty more years with you. I would give up anything, Agnes, anything, even my Sudoku puzzles, to stare into your beautiful blue eyes, the color of blue jay feathers. Love you, my dear.

Forever & always,

Your Rose

P.S. I think Nicole might be pregnant. She has that look about her. And she is drinking lots of ginger tea. I haven't said anything. Sheila was always nauseous when she was pregnant with Nicole, as were you with Sheila. Nicole must be having a girl. They say girls take your beauty, brains, and belly. I could be wrong, but I doubt it. I'll keep you posted, my love.

November 2, 2018

Dear Agnes,

It's been over a week and you're still with us, but your breathing changed today. It's very heavy and rattling. I know the time is almost here. Father Brian visits every couple of hours now. It feels weird waiting for someone to die. I'm in a bit of a mood today too. Just feeling cranky and exhausted. It's nice to have all the kids and grandkids around, but boy, they talk a lot. Your hands felt dry today, so I am heading down to the hospital gift shop to get some cocoa butter Jergens. I don't want it to be the end, Agnes. Can't we have more time? I know I keep asking you to open your eyes. I am sure you would if you could. I'll miss those feathers. Love you, my dear.

Forever & always,

Your Rose

November 3, 2018

Dear Agnes,

It happened early this morning before anyone else arrived. It was just you and me. Not unlike any other Saturday morning. Except we weren't in the all-season room drinking our coffee and watching the bird feeder. I've been sitting here since it happened. The boys, Sheila, and Nicole are on their way. They want to see you before the funeral home takes you away. It was peaceful. Father Brian had just said his morning prayer for you. We said the Hail Mary together, and then he left us. I knew the exact moment it happened. It was like I felt your soul leave your body. A wave of comfort and emotion overcame me all at once. I am glad you are not suffering anymore, but I don't want to go home. Going home without you will make it feel so final.

Thank you for opening your eyes one last time. Father Brian said it was your way of saying goodbye to me. The nurse said it was just an automatic physical response that can sometimes happen at the end. I liked the Irish priest's answer better. Your eyes looked just as beautiful as the day I met you. Remember that day? You were wearing that gorgeous blue dress with the silk buttons running down the back. It made your eyes look even brighter. I said to you then: "Your eyes remind me of the feathers of a blue jay." You smiled and told me they were your favorite bird. Even though I was newly married and you were recently engaged, I knew that we were meant to be in each other's lives. You were the blessing of my lifetime, Agnes. Love you, my dear.

Forever & always,

Your Rose

November 4, 2018

Dear Agnes,

Can you believe that Sheila wanted to put you in your pale pink suit? Nicole and I looked at her like she had two heads. I went to your closet and took out your robin egg blue Chanel suit. We both knew how much you wanted to be buried in your most expensive outfit. I remember the day you bought it. You said, "Clothing this expensive and high quality is meant to be worn for life and death. I'll be pissed if I am not buried in this beautiful suit."

I am excited to let you know that I was right. Nicole is pregnant. She doesn't know what she is having, but she's due in late spring. I still think she's having a girl. Sheila does too. The pregnancy is going well besides her nausea and exhaustion. Ethan has been the perfect husband to Nicole and has supplied the household with all proper pregnancy craving foods, including Nicole's favorite: gummy bears. A great-grandchild, Agnes! A new baby—how wonderful! It was nice to hear such good news today. It made me think about life instead of death for a little while.

Having them both here all day was nice, but it's been quiet since they left for the night. I hate this, Agnes. Your chair at the table stays untouched. Your side of the bed is empty. Your books piled on the end table are gathering dust. Your toothbrush still sits in its holder. Every corner of the house reminds me of you. You would probably tell me to stop missing you, but I wish we had more time left, Agnes. The wake is tomorrow—the funeral Tuesday. Father Brian is doing your Mass. I know you never met him, but I feel like he knows you more than Father Christopher ever cared to know. Anyway, I hope you like the Mass. I know you didn't want anyone to make a fuss about you, but you meant so much to so many people. And all of those people want to pay tribute to your beautiful life. I am making the egg biscuits and pizzelles for the reception. I've got nothing else to do so I don't mind. Plus, it will make me feel close to you. Love you, my dear.

Forever & always,

Your Rose

November 5, 2018

Dear Agnes,

I am a bit tired and drained, so I can't talk for long tonight.
A lot of people came to pay their respects today. You looked
beautiful, and peaceful too. Almost as if you were just taking
a long nap. We say our final goodbyes tomorrow, my love. I
don't want to yet. Love you, my dear.

Forever & always,

Your Rose

November 6, 2018

Dear Agnes,

The Mass was beautiful today. I think you would agree.
Father Brian's sermon was perfect. He described your death
as a ship sailing off into the horizon at sunset. He said you
had arrived home with God and now live in eternal peace.
That gave me comfort. I might go to church every Sunday
now that he's taking over at our parish. I'm sure you're
laughing at me from heaven, but I'm serious. He and I talked
daily for the past couple of weeks. I feel no judgment from
him, only love. Plus, I know I am not too far behind you. I
need to start getting in good with God to make sure I join
you in heaven when I die.

Sheila's eulogy was just perfect. It made me cry. I am pretty
sure you would have said that she should win a Pulitzer. She
has always been a beautiful writer. She even had the whole
church laughing when she told the story about the time the
bat got in the house, and you got it out by singing at it. I
almost peed my pants that day.

There was a lot of love there, Agnes. We served Italian
wedding soup at the reception per your written instructions.
And everyone was happy to have the cookies there. The
funniest thing happened, too. As Father Brian said his last
graveside prayer, a blue jay flew right over us and squawked
so loudly. We all chuckled. It made me miss you, but at the

same time, it brought me comfort. I know it's *Housewives* night, my love, but I'm exhausted. Love you, my dear.

Forever & always,

Your Rose

November 21, 2018

Dear Agnes,

I can't believe it's Thanksgiving tomorrow. I know it's been a while since we last spoke, but the kids and grandkids are driving me a bit nuts. They mean well, but they haven't left me alone for weeks. They keep me so busy during the day, and I am exhausted at night. I fall asleep as soon as I sit down. I'm sure you would say it is no different than any other night. I am feeling a little nervous about Thanksgiving. It's my first holiday without you. Not surprisingly, Sheila typed up an itinerary for the day. I told her all I wanted to do was sit down at a table, eat food, and watch some football.

I've been keeping the bird feeder full, and I've even been spreading some extra seed in the back bed for the chipmunks and squirrels like I know you like to do. I think we are the only ones in the neighborhood still filling their bird feeder because it's like Snow White's cottage in our backyard every day. Sparrows, doves, chickadees, cardinals, and blue jays. I think the life of a bird is pretty nice. They get to fly. They can perch wherever they want and soak up the sun. And they get fed by strangers without asking. I wouldn't mind that life, especially if you were a bird with me. Love you, my dear.

Forever & always,

Your Rose

December 31, 2018

Dear Agnes,

I'm so sorry I haven't written. Between Thanksgiving and Christmas it's been quite busy. Even tonight, I'm going to Sheila's to see the ball drop. Me, going to someone's house to see the ball drop on New Year's. Can you believe it? I told Sheila I would be asleep by 9 p.m. She told me I better not be. She got me some brandy to toast at midnight because she knows champagne gives me headaches.

And Sheila will definitely be getting a midnight kiss; her new boyfriend Charles will be there. We met him for the first time on Christmas Eve. What a nice guy, Agnes. You would approve. He is tall, very handsome, and half Italian. Dark hair and eyes. He grew up in Massachusetts but came here to attend Providence College and never left. Good Catholic boy, you would say. He is divorced, has two kids (both adults now), and owns his own business—don't ask me what type. Most importantly, he adores Sheila. And she loves him. The kids brought me a beautiful present for Christmas—an ornament with a hand-painted blue jay. So thoughtful. We all hung it on the Christmas tree together in honor of you.

I'm glad the holidays happened so quickly after you passed. They gave me something else to focus on. But with the winter coming, I'm a bit nervous. You know how I get all moody when the sun isn't out and there is snow on the ground. Love you, my dear.

Forever & always,

Your Rose

January 29, 2019

Dear Agnes,

It's been a harsh winter so far. There has been a lot of snow, so I have been stuck in the house. The kids and Nicole come by a few times a week, but other than that, there is not much going on to keep my mind busy. I mostly sit and watch TV.

I tried to sort through your things, but it was too hard. Nicole recommended having a family night for everyone to come and help me go through the house. She said it would be nice if everyone had a chance to pick something special of yours to remember you by. It sounded like an excellent idea at the time, but it just upset me to see everyone going through your things. I know it is all just "stuff," but that "stuff" is all I have left to remember you by. I don't want to get rid of anything. I want to keep it all. I want to open your closet and see your color-coordinated wardrobe. I want to see your porcelain angel collection sitting in the curio. And I, the lifelong Red Sox fan, even want to keep your stupid chipped Yankees mug. I couldn't help myself, but I snapped while watching them. It was just too hard, Agnes. It is too hard. I told them that this house was not a flea market. They tried to console me, but I couldn't take it anymore. I called them all selfish and told them to leave. They decided they were in no rush to clean out your things and told me to keep everything as it was for as long as I wanted. They are just trying to be helpful, and I want our children and grandchildren to have something that reminds them of you, but I just want to keep you here, close to me, always and forever.

I'm exhausted, Agnes. I'm going to lie down now. It's nice to still smell the traces of Jergens left on your pillowcase. Love you, my dear.

Forever & always,

Your Rose

February 21, 2019

Dear Agnes,

We always said February was the worst month. Even though it's the shortest, it drags on. I think it's because we love the month of March so much. Your birthday, St. Joseph's Day, daylight saving time, and what you like to call the "actual most wonderful time of the year"—Girl Scout Cookie, Easter candy, and zeppole time! Maybe I'll start to feel better next month.

I haven't gone out much to refill the bird feeder this winter. It's too cold, and it's still snowing a lot. But the most beautiful thing happened the other day. It was a particularly down day for me. I didn't even get out of my pajamas. The snow was coming down hard, so I drank my coffee in the all-season room to watch it fall on the trees. It was so pretty. But can you imagine? There were five blue jays just sitting in the tree next to the patio. Five of them! In the middle of a snowstorm! God bless those little feathers. I hope they weren't waiting for me to fill the feeder. They'll be waiting until April. They did make me feel better, however. I closed my eyes and tried to remember your eyes. It's been too long since I've seen them. For a second I wondered if you were sending me a message from heaven, but I know that's not possible, right? Love you, my dear.

Forever & always,

Your Rose

March 29, 2019

Dear Agnes,

Well, this was the worst March on record. The weather was stupid. Apparently, there is a national shortage of Cadbury Mini Eggs, and daylight saving time has my sleep schedule out of whack. I liked sleeping later in the morning, but ever since the time changed, I'm up at the crack of dawn. I finally got outside and put seed in the bird feeder, and not a single blue jay has come by yet. Just those chunky mourning doves and that stinkin' squirrel. He has now figured out a way to hang upside down from the feeder and dump the seed onto the ground. That son of a gun! I had Nicole research ways to get rid of squirrels, but it seems like a hopeless cause. I was hoping to see a blue jay on your birthday or St. Joseph's Day, but I didn't. I even did our regular St. Joseph's Day tradition. I went to Sal's Bakery and got two zeppole and a loaf of Italian bread. I made your mother's gravy recipe and I watched *The Godfather*. It was supposed to be the perfect day…except you weren't there. I lost my appetite, fell asleep during the movie, and dropped the zeppole on the kitchen floor. The day was cursed. I was so mad; it was like a rage boiling up inside me. I had the sudden urge to break something. So I took the whole bowl of nicely sauced spaghetti and threw it against the wall. It felt good, but what a pain in the ass to clean up. Couldn't you have made it special for me from heaven, Agnes? It was hard enough not to have you there, but to have my day ruined too; it just plain sucked. I even told Father Brian about it after Mass that week. He told me some bologna about not needing to see a sign and instead just knowing that you are with me.

Personally, I'd like to have a sign, thank you very much. You hear that, Agnes? Well, regardless, love you, my dear.

Forever & always,

Your Rose

April 20, 2019

Dear Agnes,

Signs of early spring are all around. Your crocuses have bloomed, and everything is becoming green again. It feels nice. Sheila brought me to the doctor a few weeks ago. He put me on a medication called Zoloft. It seems to be helping. But it could also be the longer days and warmer weather.

Nicole suggested I start some sort of project, like painting. I laughed at her and told her that I couldn't even draw a stick figure. Then, she suggested painting a room. I didn't think that was a bad idea. You're going to be annoyed, but the room I decided to paint is the all-season room. I know it is your favorite room, but Agnes, we haven't changed the color since we moved in. You said the beige was neutral. I say it's ugly. I decided to go with a lovely blue. Thomas took me to Home Depot to pick out the paint color. He insisted on coming with me instead of Sheila. He said Home Depot is a man's store. I didn't argue with him. You know how stubborn our son can be.

I never knew how many different shades of blue there were. Frankly, they all looked alike to me. Thomas was adamant they each had their own unique tone. I picked one because it reminded me of your eyes. And guess what? When Thomas and I brought the swatch up to the counter, the paint associate told us the name of the paint color was called Blue Jay. I knew right away that was the color. I finished the second coat this morning and it looks beautiful. I know you

would love it. I wish you were here with me enjoying coffee
in our newly painted all-season room. Love you, my dear.

Forever & always,

Your Rose

May 29, 2019

Dear Agnes,

I was right! Nicole had a baby girl. She is a week old and beautifully perfect. The delivery went okay. She was in labor for almost a day but pushed for only a couple of hours. Sheila is over the moon in love with her new granddaughter. I am pretty sure she bought everything in the baby section of Target.

Oh, and I almost forgot to tell you the most fantastic part. Her name! Nicole and Ethan named their baby girl Agnes Rose. Nicole said she hopes her baby girl has all the strength, beauty, kindness, and wisdom as her two great grandmothers. Isn't that just the sweetest thing you've ever heard?

Anyway, I have to go, love. Sorry I can't talk longer. Thomas is picking me up and we are all going to Nicole's. It's been two whole days since I've seen that baby. I need my fix! Love you, my dear.

Forever & always,

Your Rose

June 28, 2019

Dear Agnes,

It's official! Our kids have gone crazy. You're going to die—well, technically, you already are dead, but you know what I mean. Anyway, our children bought me a dog! They said that a dog is a good companion and can help me deal with losing you and being alone. Frankly, I was kind of getting used to being left alone. It was nice and quiet around the house. Now, there is this brown and white dopey hound dog who barks at every little sound and requires me to pick up after him all the time. He is cute and all, but he is certainly no replacement for you. Although he doesn't talk back to me, so he does have that over you. Ha! I decided to name him Leo, after Leonardo da Vinci. Let's see if he lives up to his name. So far, he seems pretty stupid. Love you, my dear.

Forever & always,

Your Rose

July 17, 2019

Dear Agnes,

This summer royally sucks! It has been too hot and humid to do anything. I try to walk Leo around the block, but it feels like I'm swimming in clam chowder with every step I take. Even Leo is done with the gross weather. I tried to teach him how to play fetch in the backyard, but he hasn't figured it out yet. He will run after the ball, but instead of picking it up and bringing it back to me, he plops himself down on the lawn next to the damn ball—lazy dog. I can't say that I blame him. So instead of being outdoors, we have been watching lots of crime documentaries on Netflix. I am not sure Leo is into the shows, but he is certainly into all the belly and head pats I give him while we watch. My birthday is in less than a month. I hope this humidity comes to an end soon. I don't want my birthday to be ruined the way your birthday was this year. Well, anyway, I wanted to say a quick hello to you. It's almost 6:30 pm, so I have to run now. You know how I have to watch Lester Holt every night. Love you, my dear.

Forever & always,

Your Rose

August 10, 2019

Dear Agnes,

I had the most wonderful birthday today! Nicole and Sheila came over and surprised me with such a thoughtful gift. Last week, they called me and told me to be ready on Saturday by noon and dress to impress. I hadn't dressed up since your funeral. I was excited to put some heels and makeup on. They gave me a small gift box wrapped in beautiful blue and white polka-dotted paper when they arrived. Inside was a silver blue jay brooch. Nicole said I no longer have to worry about looking for a blue jay wherever I go because you will always be with me as long as I wear this brooch. I immediately teared up and clipped it to my silk blazer. They took me out to lunch at a fancy restaurant on Federal Hill, and then we went to the matinee showing of *Hamilton*. I felt like a kid all over again, Agnes. I've wanted to see it ever since we saw that video clip of Lin-Manuel Miranda at the White House. He is such a talented guy. And the show did not disappoint. It was beautiful. I learned so much too. They never taught us that history in school.

I wish you could have been there, my love, but it really was a wonderful day. Our children are very special. But wait, the best part of the day happened later in the evening. Leo and I were watching TV when I had a craving for something sweet. I dug through the cabinets and couldn't find anything, so I decided to move everything around in the freezer just in case there was an old pint of ice cream. There wasn't. But I found something else, even better than the delicious bite of cake I had at lunch—the last of the Thin Mint cookies you hid last year! I ate the entire sleeve. Thank you for the wonderful birthday treat, Agnes. Love you, my dear.

Forever & always,

Your Rose

September 23, 2019

Dear Agnes,

I babysat Agnes Rose today. She is so precious. Nicole had to go back to work but can do a four-day schedule instead of five. Sheila watches Agnes Rose twice a week and Ethan's mom the other two. Sheila had to go for her annual mammogram today, so I watched the baby for a few hours while Sheila went to her appointment. Leo likes the baby. He laid in front of her rocking seat while she slept and just stared at her. Whenever she moved or made a noise, he got right up to make sure she was okay. It was the absolute cutest. It felt so nice to have a baby in my arms again. Her skin is soft, and her eyes are blue, just like yours. When I had to change her diaper, I was reminded that not all of the stuff with babies is fun. I was glad to have Sheila come back to relieve me. Being responsible for Leo is more than enough. The leaves are starting to turn all different shades. The giant oak tree in the backyard is now in its deep yellow stage—your favorite. I miss you, Agnes, every day. Although I feel a bit happier and lighter than just a few months ago, I still wish you were here. Love you, my dear.

Forever & always,

Your Rose

October 20, 2019

Dear Agnes,

It is hard to believe that in only a couple of weeks, you will
have been gone for an entire year—365 days without you,
but I've survived it.

Your pillow no longer smells like Jergens, and I packed
away some of your clothes last week. I donated your books
to the community library. And I gave all of the kids and
grandkids a porcelain angel. Don't worry, I did keep a few
for me too. I was finally able to throw your toothbrush out,
and I can now sit in your chair at the table.

I still talk to you pretty much every day. It's funny because
sometimes I just feel you. A wave of warmth comes over me.
I say hello out loud to you and smile. I place my hand on my
brooch and close my eyes. I picture your blue eyes and feel
safe. On those days, I'll find myself puttering around doing
something, and when I look around, there, in a tree, is a blue
jay.

Ironically, this is the last page of the journal. I guess Nicole
knows her stuff. We are going to the flea market today to
look around and get lunch, apparently from trucks and not a
restaurant. Maybe I'll pick up a journal while I am there, my
love. Love you, my dear.

Forever & always,

Your Rose

Ends

by
C.H. Kim

"Sur, you really shouldn't have. Too thoughtful, too kind." Mama placed the gifts on the crooked side table and carefully set the shoddy wrapping paper on the ground. The wrapping paper, a recycled grocery bag, was turned inside out to hide the supermarket's branding. A mild-mannered fire crackled in the fireplace, reaching for the bag with a lackluster effort.

"Do you think Mama actually has the time to read?" Sol scoffed. "What a waste of money."

"Not like Sur has to be careful with money. They've got an Office job," Sim said.

Sur looked down and noticed their shiny shoes reflecting the apathetic flames.

Mama gently placed her hands on Sur's arm. "I appreciate the gifts, especially the cream. It'll help after long shifts in the Field." She massaged her stiff hands.

The clock on the wall ticked louder and louder until everyone took their cues to turn in for the night. After kissing Mama on the cheek and giving each sibling an obligatory side hug, Sur gathered their belongings and slipped quietly into the night.

At that late hour only a few others stood on the platform, sleepily awaiting the next train. Sur looked again at their shoes and shuffled their feet self-consciously. *Well, I need these shoes. Otherwise I wouldn't fit in at the Office, right? It's not my fault Sol and Sim have poor taste.*

On the train Sur found a spot to stand in front of one of the small screens that displayed cheesy ads for local businesses, frustratingly easy trivia questions, and the same snippets of news for three days in a row. Sur watched anyway.

"*...that the value of the Product has skyrocketed in the past quarter. This has led to exports of the Product running on a 24/7 schedule, with increased demands for labor from the Downcity, Pell, and Salma Districts. However, not everyone approves of—*"

The clip briefly cut out. In the silence one of the passengers sobbed into her cell phone. Sur averted their eyes back to the screen, which, after a few seconds of glitching, returned to a trivia question asking how many stomachs a cow has. Sur picked at a fading sticker on the door until the train arrived at their stop.

***

By the time Sur had eaten breakfast and brewed a batch of coffee, the sunrise peeked over the surrounding concrete buildings. It shone through the humble square window and onto the clock on the opposite wall. They were already running late, so Sur added one more bowl to the threatening pile of dishes in the sink. *After work, for sure.*

Outside, the streets bustled with workers on their way to the Field dressed in cargo coveralls and smocks that might as well have been identical, save for the logos embroidered on the left side of the chest. Some workers were retiring after a long graveyard shift, their well-worn boots shuffling on the smooth pavement.

With practiced movements, Sur weaved between hundreds of kiosks selling flashy Personalizers and booths that advertised positions for Field workers. The banners

104

read, *Reliable pay*, *No experience necessary!*, and *More jobs for locals.*

Recruiters monitored the streets, hungry for a fresh face, for someone unaware of what followed the signing of a contract.

Since the discovery of the Product, opportunists had flocked to the small Town. The Town leaders seized the chance to get the Town on the map. Before anyone could object, the export of the Product through an ever-growing network of Pipes was bringing prosperity to the otherwise modest burg. Sur had started out in the Field, spending grueling hours attaching one metal Pipe to the next. Their acumen and potential for leadership had earned them a more suitable position in the Office—better pay, no hard labor.

The distant sound of drilling and clanking played a never-ending soundtrack for all passersby. The web of Pipes below the surface pumped and whooshed along to the rhythm.

Sur arrived at the Office, clocked in, and settled at their desk. While Sur waited for the computer to boot up, they straightened up a few items: a family photo from three summers ago, their gold-trimmed *Research and Design Manager* nameplate, and a neglected succulent that could have been dead or alive. The computer powered on to a nondescript blue background with a handful of folders on the desktop. Sur twiddled their thumbs before clicking on the folder named "Delta Deep." Several blueprints and spreadsheets featuring detailed calculations popped up on the screen.

There was a knock on the wall behind Sur's desk.

"Hey, you're here."

Sur looked up to find Eden peering over the cubicle separator. The fluorescent lights of the minimalist office space glinted off her smart glasses.

"Did you hear about what happened in the Pell District?"

"No, what happened?" Sur asked, scratching the nape of their neck.

Eden glanced sideways. "One of their main Pipes burst in the middle of the night. Fourteen workers died, and they lost a shit ton of Product."

"Holy shit," Sur whispered.

"I know, right? Something hasn't been sitting right with me. It's like—"

The Supervisor strolled into Sur's cubicle. "Do you have a moment to chat?" The light reflected off his bald head as he cocked his chin to the side.

Eden cleared her throat and slowly sat back down at her own desk.

"Uh, yeah. Certainly." As if they were going to say no.

The Supervisor led them back to his workroom and pulled out a file with a familiar title written on the front. "It seems as if we need to expedite Delta Deep, considering last night's…tragic accident. The public will, of course, want to know what steps will be taken to prevent another…tragic accident. It's imperative that they are given the chance to grieve the fourteen lost. In fact, this might even boost morale for the project in the long run. But they mustn't linger on it. They might forget why we started this project in the first place, and that would be bad news for the Town's recent successes. You understand, yes?"

And before they knew it, Sur had agreed to work overtime.

"So, what was that about?" Eden nudged.

"Nothing."

"Nothing?"

"Will you stay late with me until I'm done?"

Eden sighed. "Fine, but you're buying dinner."

At the end of the night Sur and Eden clocked out and shimmied into their coats. They headed down the main road towards their usual spot, Nice to Eat You. It was one of the only restaurants left that still served actual food rather than the hyper-efficient gastronomic experiments everyone else ate. *Ate* wasn't even the right word for something that was more akin to fueling up at a gas station. As they neared the end of the block, Eden stopped in her tracks.

"Do you feel that?"

There was no need for a response. The ground erupted into violent shaking. Eden and Sur grasped each other and then a nearby lamppost. Seconds later, sirens wailed in every direction.

"What the hell was that?" Sur stammered.

"I knew it. I fucking knew it," Eden said. "They said it was going to happen like this. We need to get out of here."

"What are you talking about?"

"They—the articles said eventually it'll all collapse." She paced back and forth, her eyes darting from one lamppost to the next.

"Eden, did you even fact check those? Earthquakes are natural disasters, you know."

"Key word: disaster. And when was the last time you remembered an earthquake in this part of the country?"

Sur rolled their eyes. "It happens! You can't freak out about every little thing, Eden. It's not good for you. It doesn't help anybody."

"Will you just walk me back to my place?" Eden asked.

The walk to Eden's apartment was eerily hushed. The post-quake commotion had quickly dissipated and the symphony of Pipes had taken over once more.

Sur worried about Eden. They felt bad about their condescending choice of words, but she was prone to fantastic ideas and conspiracy theories. They had really come to care about their coworker—no, friend—at a time when the only people who really understood you were the ones who were nine-to-fiveing it beside you.

When the two of them arrived at the apartment, Sur placed a firm hand on Eden's shoulder. "Promise to get some sleep, okay?"

Sur waited on the platform for the next train. Their phone buzzed in their pocket.

"Hi Mama, how are you?"

"Honey, are you alright? Did you feel the earthquake where you were too?"

"Yeah, Mama. I'm fine."

"Sol and Sim are saying we shouldn't go to work in the Field tomorrow. They're saying it's connected to the Product, and it might be dangerous to go to work." The news droned in the background on the family's TV.

"It's fine, Mama. Don't listen to them. I was just reading an article on my phone before you called that said it was an isolated incident."

Mama's patient, labored breathing came through the other end of the line. "Okay, baby. You're right. You're so smart. I trust you. You know I love you."

"I love you too, Mama. I'll try and stop by this weekend."

***

Oh crap. Sur sat up in bed and looked at the clock. They had forgotten to do the dishes last night again. And they were running late. Again.

The workers in the streets hurried. The recruiters hunted. The machinery hummed. Sur swore they heard the Pipes stop for a second, one or two hiccups in the mechanic melody.

Eden, who was usually at the Office a few minutes early, was not at her desk. Sur recalled the events from last night. *Probably had a panic attack and stayed home. I'll call later.*

Sur was excited at the thought of launching Delta Deep. It wasn't just about making Pipe ends meet; it was about instantaneous, effective delivery of Product. Maybe the improvements to the extraction process could shift the focus to refinement and manufacturing. Maybe the companies could pay their Field workers more and Mama could retire soon.

Sur had been so wrapped up in the project they hadn't even noticed it was time for lunch. They sat alone in the lounge. Everybody else had finished eating within the first three minutes of lunch period, chugging nutrition mixtures from their sleek stainless-steel canisters cased in various Personalizers. The Supervisor had one with the company logo, and Sur's coworker Tian had one that said *This definitely ISN'T wine!*; it made them shudder every time. They retrieved a container of pork and rice from the derelict microwave and made plans to visit Eden's apartment after work.

Eden's apartment building was possibly more decrepit than the microwave in the lounge, but she insisted on the close commute and the potential property value. The kiosk outside her building sold cell phone Personalizers from three seasons ago, not that Sur cared much. Still, it was a turnoff. When Sur got to Eden's door on the sixteenth floor, they heard anxious shuffling.

"Eden?"

The shuffling paused momentarily and the door clicked open. Eden's chic and usually organized living room was strewn with several half-filled bags and boxes.

Without making eye contact, she said, "Sur, I'm leaving."

"Leaving? Eden, what are you talking about?" They leaned against the doorpost. "Is this about last night? Did you get some sleep? Did you take your meds?"

Eden's face tensed and then relaxed. "I know what it looks like, but you have to trust me. Pack your stuff and come with me. Shit's about to hit the fan." She turned around to continue filling a box with her books. "I just know it."

"What are you even talking about? Where are you going to go? I can't just leave my mom."

"I'm going north, moving away from the Town. We would need to find different work, but it's possible. We're both smart."

"Eden, there's nothing north of us. It's all forests and rural shit. What are you going to do—become a farmhand?"

"It doesn't fucking matter, Sur! We need to leave!"

"I can't do it. I'm sorry."

The terse apology snuffed out any warmth that might have issued from the apartment's arthritic radiator.

"I need you here with me," Sur said.

"There won't be a you or a me if we don't get out of here." Eden opened her arms as if to invite Sur in and pull them closer.

Sur didn't budge.

"Okay, well…well, I guess this is the part where I say you'll always have a place to stay if you change your mind." Eden left it at that and went back to packing.

Sur barely remembered taking the train home. Shoes off, keys on the hook, briefcase against the bookshelf, phone on the counter, dishes in the sink. Dishes. Sur only had dishes in the sink because of their outdated convictions about real food. Was it worth it? Couldn't they just drink the nutrition mixture like all of the other Office workers?

Sur skipped dinner and went straight to bed. They texted their mom asking if they should bring anything for tomorrow, but of course Mama politely refused.

Eden must be on her way now. I'm really going to miss her. Sur pulled the blanket over their head to block out the streetlights. *What if she's right?*

***

"Mama, you're going to hurt yourself!"

"You may be the brains of the family, but I can still fix just about anything in this house," Mama chirped as she climbed down the rickety ladder. She seemed especially sprightly this afternoon, but Sur didn't buy it for one second. Sol had pulled Sur aside earlier to tell them about Mama's leg problem, and they had been keeping a keen eye on it all day.

"I need to get going so I can catch the last train."

"Shouldn't you be able to afford your own transportation, o' mighty Office worker?" Sim taunted from the breakfast nook.

Sur didn't bother to address the comment, put on their coat, and walked towards Mama's bedroom. The room was small, but the light streaming through the lacy drapes created an ethereal, dreamy atmosphere. Sur reached into their coat pocket to pull out a hefty envelope of money to leave on Mama's nightstand. As they were about to set the envelope down, Sur noticed the book they had given Mama had a bookmark about one-third of the way through. They gave the envelope a quick kiss and turned it over so the small hand-drawn heart on the seam was facing up.

***

Today was the big day. The team was ready to launch Delta Deep. It had been a month since Eden left. Sur had tried calling her a few times but she never picked up. They would have wanted to celebrate with a feast, but since Eden was gone, Sur accepted the Office-sponsored celebration in the lounge. Sur wanted to express their thanks to the Supervisor for giving them the opportunity to work on the project but couldn't find him.

"Has anyone seen the Supervisor?"

"I haven't seen the Supervisor all day, actually," Tian said.

Fil, Eden's replacement, spoke up. "I saw him in his workroom yesterday. He basically spent the whole day in there talking to some higher-up. It sounded rough, but any person who misses the only fun day at work has got to be a weirdo."

Might as well have a drink. Sur floated around the beverage table and tapped their foot along to the music.

A man in a gray herringbone suit with an electric purple necktie and caterpillar eyebrows approached Sur. He set his cup down and motioned for Sur to follow him just outside the lounge door. He closed the door behind him and introduced himself, raising his voice just above the chatter of the party.

"I'm the Executive. And you are Sur, correct?" Before Sur could respond in full, he continued. "The company loves your work with Delta Deep and would like to offer you the position of Supervisor."

"I don't understand. I thought each branch only employed one Supervisor, and we already—"

"Yes, and that would be you. Think about it." The Executive turned on his heels, re-entered the party, and left Sur with a sinister shovel in their hands, unsure if they were digging the Supervisor's grave or their own.

They dialed Mama's number. It rang nine times before going to voicemail. They dialed Sol, Sim, and even Eden. Nothing.

Fil opened the door. "Hey! You're missing out!"

"Right." Sur sighed. *I'll call back later for sure.*

The lively buzz in the lounge had pacified to a lull. Most had exhausted their conversations about the newest season of toilet and bathtub Personalizers, and some resigned to mindlessly watching the news on the TV. The anchors recited financial-success-this, booming-economy-that.

The screen abruptly switched to a bright crimson background. The words *URGENT ALERT* appeared. A harrowing siren blared through the Office on all devices. In the midst of the crisis, Sur only caught the words *giant sinkhole* and *mass evacuation* before Tian grabbed them by the collar on the way towards the door.

The Office workers flew down the staircases and out into the streets. Sur couldn't breathe. The collapsing buildings kicked up so much dust and debris that it coated the inside of their mouth and nose. A limb peeked out from under a concrete pillar. People writhed on the floor in piles of rubble. Instinctively, Sur rushed to the train station.

Mama? Why didn't Mama pick up her phone? Did the sinkhole start in the Field? The Field is east of the Town. The tears streaming from their eyes mixed with the soot on their face. *Train. Westbound. Eden saw this coming. I should have just taken Mama with me. We could have all gone together.* By the time they reached the station, Sur's face was caked with a grayish brown mud.

People scrambled to get into the packed cars. There was shrieking, wailing, and sobbing but nobody was saying anything. Cell phones were out, dialing and ringing to no avail. The rumbling of the earth roared in their eardrums, and, in the blink of an eye, whole buildings disappeared. In another blink, Sur took off on the very last train out of the Town.

***

"Today marks the one-year anniversary of the tragedy of Delta Deep, what we now know was a massive sinkhole formed by the unabated mining and export of the Product. Experts claim the corporations knew the excavation's long-lasting impacts would—"

"Can you turn that off?" Sur snapped.

"Happy happy, mate. Didn't realize that was going to set you off," Ike replied. Ike, a lanky man with a fiery beard, was Sur's working partner in the Field.

Sur stared daggers into Ike and went back to eating their lunch. Lunch breaks for Field workers were brief and unpleasant, but working grueling hours in the Field was decidedly worse. After Delta Deep failed, Sur and thousands of other Office workers relocated to the City. Their only opportunities to start anew were in Field jobs.

Ike placed his knobby hands on the table and leaned in a few inches closer.

"For the last time, Ike, I don't want to talk about it."

"But ya have to be at least a little scared of it happening again. I need ta know for my own safety!" Ike threw his hands up, gesturing to delineate the invisible bubble around his body.

"First of all, we're far, far away from my Town, and the business is different here." Sur gave their nutrition canister an agitated shake. "If the sinkhole formed because of exporting Product, then we wouldn't have that problem if we're connecting Pipes for importing Product. It's common sense, right?"

"Okay, smarty pants! You got me." Ike ran his fingers over his furrowed brow, leaving a streak of grease on his forehead.

"Besides, that wouldn't happen here. There's been too much development in the neighboring districts for companies to risk their investments like that. It's a bigger City, so we're safe." Sur relaxed their shoulders, nervous about losing their temper in front of the lunchroom security camera. The two of them absentmindedly stared at the silver clock hanging next to the security camera as it menacingly counted down the end of their break.

Eden had been right. Sur tried messaging her again after the disaster, but the number now belonged to a man named Bos, who attempted to sell Sur a Personalizer for trash cans. All of the major directories came up empty whenever Sur typed in Eden's name. *Where exactly did she go and why didn't she ever pick up?* Mama, Sol, and Sim had also been promptly removed from any directories, along with all of the other Field workers who were caught in the sinkhole that day.

Mama, I'm sorry. I'm so sorry.

"Alright, folks! You know today's the big day!" The Forewoman spoke into the microphone and rubbed her hands together. "We have gathered here to put in place the final ceremonial Pipe into our City, a City whose citizens have worked tirelessly to make good things happen for all people." Several of the Field workers cheered, standing around the mouth of the Pipe that fed into the open basin. The City had long anticipated the imports—and resulting benefits—that would come with the completion of the Pipeline.

"Here we go!" The Forewoman pulled a cartoonishly large lever. Sur watched the mouth of the Pipe; it grinned, almost mischievously, as the ground began to rumble. Sur closed their eyes and took three deep breaths. The crowd reveled in the rumbling, jumping up and down like schoolchildren.

Ike plugged his nose. "My God, what is that stench?"

Everyone else did the same, looking around for an explanation. The rancid odor grew more offensive with every passing second. Some people started to retch. The Forewoman's smile eventually splintered into a grimace, and she hastily covered her face with her grubby hands.

"Look!" someone shouted, pointing at the Pipe's opening.

Flowing out of the Pipe and pouring into the basin came the Waste.

Negative Space

by
Lou Blair

CW: Gore, Animal Death

Maude stepped out onto the beach, eir boot sinking into dry sand. The cove before em simmered in the hot spring sun. Though not yet at the lethal temperatures of summer, the beach still roasted with waves of heat like a glaze of oil in the distance, the sun's light bright enough to blind. Bordered by looming cliffs that stretched into the sea, the area was quite private, accessible only by boat or a small tunnel through the caves through which Maude had arrived. Likely popular during the milder months of winter, the little cove sat empty in the heat. Nothing suggested people had ever been there at all, save for a single weathered towel caught on a piece of driftwood. It snapped in the breeze, colors faded to white and glowing from months under the sun.

Maude observed it all through the visor of eir helmet, its lens tinged violet and designed to dim the burning light of the sun. On days like today, it emphasized the dark points of the world and provided Maude the protection ey needed to do eir work. Ey knelt to the ground and surveyed the tracks left in the sand. A seabird's small, stick-like prints. Natural ripples left from the tide. Nothing matched that which ey sought—a runaway panther-dog smuggled onto the planet and mishandled to the point of escape. Bounty hunters would take care of the smugglers—Maude was only there to retrieve the stray and bring it home.

A cave marked the far side of the beach. It was small and craggy, but big enough for a large animal to hide in. Maude headed toward it, cataloging eir supplies as ey went. Steel cable rope, strapped across eir back—check. First-aid kit, stocked for humans and animals—check. Boots, pants, jacket—ey patted emself down—check, check, check.

Ey hesitated as eir palms brushed eir sides. The knife sheathed against the small of eir back nosed at the edge of eir mind, its ever-present weight a buzz in Maude's head. Everything else ey had left behind. Working with wild animals tended to get dicey, so jobs encouraged eir minimalism. The less stuff ey brought with em, the less ey could break or lose.

The mouth of the cave revealed a deeper, darker cavern than Maude had first thought. Ey stood at the entrance and stuck eir hands in eir pockets, peering inside.

"Hello?" ey called. A small splash sounded toward the back. Ey stepped inside the cave and changed the dial on eir helmet. In the green of eir night vision, ey saw that the cave twisted toward the back to create a hidden alcove.

"If the panther-dog is hearing this," Maude continued, "I'm here to bring you home."

The panther-dog growled, the sound tinny through Maude's helmet.

"And I'm more than happy to wait you out," ey added, taking a seat next to one of the tide pools.

No answer from the panther-dog.

Sheltered now by the cool shade of the cave, ey removed eir helmet and took a replenishing breath of sea air. Ey shook out eir hair a bit and leaned over one of the tide pools to poke around at the creatures inside. Maude looked at eir hands. Bitten-down nails and dry skin. Ey pushed back eir greasy, curly hair. It brushed eir shoulders now, loose and ticklish. Ey blew eir bangs out of eir face and sat back.

Ey had only showered once since ey had killed the fox-eaglet.

Ey were cutting apart the wire fence it was trapped in when it turned on em, wrenched its wings free and knocked em down. Taloned paws drew blood from Maude's shoulders. A juvenile, it already touted the likeness of a gryphon with its golden-orange feathers that shone in the daylight, its broken wings dashed with bright blood.

The knife was in Maude's hand before the beak made it to eir jugular. Hot blood sprayed eir face before ey could process eir strike.

Maude cleared eir throat and called to the panther-dog.

"It's just you and me, buddy. I know you're scared, but I just wanna help you get home, alright?"

Ey got to eir feet and took a piece of rope in eir hands.

"And I'm pretty good at this, so let's not—"

A high-pitched ring pierced the air, sharp and aching. Ey clamped eir hands over eir ears and clenched eir teeth against the pain. Ey briefly suspected the panther-dog, perhaps as some mutated defense mechanism Maude had never heard of, but the sound was distinctly inorganic. It was almost machine-like in the way it ground and grated in waves, spiking in Maude's head like a migraine.

Ey looked around for its source, but saw nothing. It had to be outside. Ey strained to hear anything else, but caught only the panther-dog's whines and howls. Heart twinging at its pain, ey moved toward the back of the cave to help.

The ring cut short as quickly as it came. Maude tentatively lowered eir hands, then threw them up again as the panther-dog tore out of the shadows. It bowled em over and raced for the mouth of the cave, careened off its rocky edge, then disappeared out into the light.

"Shit—" Maude scrambled back into eir helmet and onto eir feet and sprinted out after eir charge. The heat of the beach smothered eir body and ey stumbled. Eir boots slipped in the sand as ey went, slowing eir pursuit. Ey watched as the beast ran the length of the beach, then skittered and crashed into the cliffside. It paced and wailed for a moment, pawing at the stone, then turned and ran toward the sea. It jumped back in surprise when its paws touched the surf, yelped, and padded in circles.

They blinded you. Something inside Maude iced over. Panther-dogs were not violent creatures. They were big, lazy cats that loved company and forests. But scare anything badly enough and it will show its defense.

Fox-eagles weren't violent either. The creature had gotten snared in an old wire fence near the end of someone's property, on a wooded planet far from Maude's beach. Its wings were caught in rusted metal and feathers bent in all wrong directions. Maude approached it with gentle hands and sweet murmurs, but when eir shears clipped part of its wing, it panicked.

The beast was bigger and stronger than Maude and tipped em over easily. Blood sprayed as it tore itself free, numbed to pain by its own fear. Maude had expected it to flee, as most of its kind would, but instead it snapped at em.

It took a chunk out of eir ribs, then nearly bit off a finger before Maude snatched eir hand away for the knife at eir hip.

Afterward, the fox-eagle lay in a soft heap, feathers and fur made heavy and small.

Maude knelt like a giant at its side. Ey sobbed for it. Eir chest ached and eir hands shook, its blood a mark upon eir skin.

Maude didn't collect the money. The job was finished, but as soon as ey reached the black of space ey turned off the engine and let emself drift.

For weeks ey coasted. Ey ate instant meals and opened books but didn't read them. Ey thought of the snap of sharp beaks and desperate cries of pain. Eir ears rang with the silence that followed.

The blade lived under a metal crate in the cargo hold, where it had clattered after Maude cast it aside. Ey took no jobs after the fox-eagle, not until the panther-dog pinged into eir inbox. A creature smuggled onto the planet that never rests, and left there to die.

Maude had thought about leaving the blade where it hid, but couldn't. It was the only one ey had. This time ey tucked it into a sheath at the small of eir back. Ey tugged eir hair into something of a knot and typed a destination into eir navigator.

Paradise. The heat-soaked planet called on Maude frequently. In the off-season it was a dumping ground for pets and beasts of all kinds, and Maude had long become familiar with the planet's inhabitants. Furred and feathered things did well under the sun, even if they weren't from Paradise to begin with. Most non-native things died during the summer, but spring and autumn allowed for some wiggle room.

There was legal animal transportation there, of course, but most of it happened illicitly. Transporting animals during the hot months of the year required blinders, else the creatures burned their retinas in the light. The smugglers had either forgone blinders completely or had done it poorly enough that the panther-dog was able to wriggle free of them once it was loose.

Maude watched the panther-dog tremble in the tide, newly blind and surrounded by unfamiliar territory. Ey clenched eir jaw and made for the beast, eir rage for the smugglers boiling down into love for the creature.

This was the whole reason ey did eir job. As much as ey wanted to see the culprits burn, it wasn't about that. Lost creatures deserving to be found, stolen creatures trying to go home—Maude helped them all. It wasn't very lucrative, but it filled Maude's heart in a way nothing else did. The thought of some creature left behind to die—it wasn't something Maude could walk away from.

Maude approached the panther-dog slowly, rope over eir shoulder and eir hands free. Up close, the beast was extraordinary. At least six feet tall at the shoulder and rippling with muscle, the panther-dog sported a blue-black pelt shot with russet—undoubtedly what had caught the smugglers' eyes. The head was mostly panther-shaped, but with a longer, more wolf-like snout. Rounded ears twitched as Maude approached. The beast tensed in anticipation and dropped into a crouch. It bared its yellow teeth, daggers as long as Maude's hand.

When Maude got too close, it jerked back and ey flinched. Ey reached instinctively for eir knife, but just as ey touched it, the cat trilled and settled, its paws kneading at the sand.

Guilt filled Maude's stomach. Ey should have left the knife behind after all. The fact ey brought it on the fox-eagle job in the first place—a *weapon*—showed ey were unfit for the job. Ey were supposed to *save* animals. Not hurt them. A little hostility was part of the deal, yet ey continued to treat them as threats.

Maude's disgust eased with a twitch of the panther-dog's ears. Ey couldn't help but grin at the beauty before em.

"Don't startle, sweetheart," Maude said softly. Ey flicked eir gaze up to meet the creature's and were greeted by big glazed-over pools irreversibly scarred by the sun.

"I just want to help. Not take you somewhere you don't belong, all right? Just back home." Maude stepped into the surf and reached out a hand. The panther-dog sniffed at it, up along eir arm until it got to eir face. It jumped when it met metal, groaning in the back of its throat and backing up. This time, Maude didn't reach for the blade.

"No, no, no, it's okay," ey said. Ey squeezed eir eyes shut against the sun and tugged off eir helmet, then dropped it at eir feet. The intensity of the sun on eir face was immediate, no longer blocked by the thin barrier of eir helmet. The wind was nothing against the sun's fire, bright and harsh against eir eyelids. Blindness lurked as a vibrant red glow just beyond that thin layer of skin, but Maude shoved eir fear aside.

The panther-dog snuffled at eir face. A wet nose bumped against Maude's forehead.

"See?" ey said, smiling. "I'm just a little creature like yourself. I can't see in this sun either."

The panther-dog chuffed and chirped at em, flicking its whiskers against Maude's face as it started to relax.

Maude eased out eir rope and slowly looped it around the beast's neck, working only by touch. The panther-dog jumped at the feeling, and its fear-growl kicked up again, but Maude soothed it with a firm hand against its neck. Ey murmured to it as ey tied, promised deep forests and quiet nights. When ey finished, ey gave its velvety nose a gentle pet. It chuffed at em and purred. Maude relaxed as ey wrapped the lead around eir hand, relieved to now be working with a giant kitten. Eir guilt rose once more, but ey shoved it down. Eir mind wandered to how ey were going to convince the animal to come back through the tunnel when the rope tore from eir hands, the tail of it slithering off eir wrist too quick to catch.

"Now don't be like that—" Maude reached out for the lead. Eir fingertips brushed fur before a violent ripping sound shocked Maude's senses. A hot, wet spatter sprayed eir face and ey jerked back and tripped over eir helmet. The impact with the ground knocked the wind out of em and left em immobile.

Silence.

Maude struggled to regain eir breath. Ey felt blindly for eir helmet, then for the panther-dog, but eir fingers grasped at nothing but burning sand. Ey must have kicked eir helmet out of reach. Panic rose in eir chest. Ey didn't dare open eir eyes against the sun—already its blistering heat brought a flush to eir cheeks. Eir skin would have dried out if not for the wetness on eir face. Ey felt at it, sticky and slick against eir fingers. Too slippery to be seawater.

Carefully, ey crawled up the beach, away from the tide and into dry sand. The hot grains pressed into eir hands and rubbed them raw, but ey couldn't risk standing up.

Something was wrong on this beach.

Eir knees met wetness. Ey frowned and felt around, expecting a trapped pool of water. Instead, eir fingers met fur. Maude's stomach dropped.

The panther-dog.

Ey located its head, heavy and still against the sand. Ey touched the soft fur of its nose, but felt no breath. Ey searched for an injury, eir shaking fingers sliding down its neck and flank…

Fur gave way to meat. Maude held down a gag as slop and organs squished under eir hands. From the ribs down, the panther-dog had been eviscerated, ground into pulp and seeping into the sand in a sick halo of gore. Maude didn't wonder what ey had been sprayed with anymore. Blood soaked the sand beneath em. Its metallic stench filled the air and mingled with the brine of the ocean. Maude laid a hand on what was left of the animal's flank and dug eir fingers into its fur.

There was no saving it.

Hot tears dripped down eir cheeks, mixing with the wet already there. Ey imagined shiny tear-tracks and smears of blood, a meager vision compared to what ey imagined for the panther-dog. Ey were grateful to be spared the actual visual.

Death was not new to Maude. Even when it came at eir hands, death was a part of life. But not like this. Never this kind of hurt. At least Maude had been quick. Ey thought of eir eaglet pup, its bloodstained feathers stuck between the chain links of the fence and Maude's knife in matching red, dropped into the grass.

Teeth clenched around a sob, Maude stood and turned toward the rest of the cove.

There was something else on this beach.

The sun had shifted to leave em partly in shadow, sheltered by the towering cliffs. The shade was a brief reprieve from the scorching sun, but it wasn't enough for em to open eir eyes. Instead, ey strained eir senses, searching for any sound, any movement in the sand.

The silence continued.

Fear grew in eir belly.

As Maude took a tentative step forward, the ringing crashed back into em and filled the cove with violent grinding waves of sound. Pain split through Maude's head, a thousand times more intense than in the cave. Ey crumpled to the ground and clutched at eir ears. Eir jaw snapped shut and caught the side of eir tongue.

As blood filled eir mouth, a heavy presence crept over em, hot and vibrating with energy. The musky smell of animal flooded Maude's nose. Eir instincts shouted *beast beast beast* and *get the fuck out of there!* Adrenaline filled eir chest as ey imagined a gaping maw above em, packed with the teeth needed to do *that* kind of destruction to a panther-dog.

With eyes squeezed shut and hands clamped over eir ears, Maude kicked out. Eir foot connected with something firm and thick. Ey struggled to eir feet, muscles tensed to run until ey realized how totally and completely fucked ey were, and ey hesitated.

No helmet, no senses, no backup.

Maude's panic grew.

Across a heartbeat, ey decided to run. Without eir helmet, ey needed somewhere ey could see, and ey needed it fast. Maude took off in the direction ey hoped the cave was. The creature had rallied by now and was gaining on em, its presence stifling and rushing closer.

Maude made it only a few steps before eir foot caught on something solid and ey went down. Unable to throw out eir hands, ey connected face-first with smooth metal. Ey cried out as eir nose crunched and eir eyes flew open. A glimpse of gray sand with searing white light at the edges was all ey saw before ey shut eir eyes tight again. Bright spots danced against eir eyelids and eir eyes watered.

Maude groped for what ey had fallen on. The ringing sound intensified as ey dropped a hand from eir ears. By a stroke of luck, eir fingers closed around the edge of eir helmet. Ey shoved it on with a roar of pain as the edge mashed eir broken nose. Ey flipped onto eir back, mouth and nose stinging, hands raised against teeth, and opened eir eyes.

But there was nothing.

The bright spots on eir eyelids faded as ey looked around. The beast had vanished, and along with it the agonizing ringing. The silence was a sudden, encompassing void that left Maude untethered.

Ey sat up and looked around. The entire beach was washed out in bright white, the sea and sand indecipherable from one another. Maude felt around on the side of eir helmet for the dial setting. It stuck fast when ey tried to turn it, caught between high sun and night vision. Ey whimpered and pressed eir lips together to hold back eir tears. Ey must have damaged it when ey broke eir goddamned face on it. Now ey could see only by the negative space of shade.

Maude located the towel by the jump of its shadow. Despite its movement, it made no sound and Maude felt no wind. The air hung still and undisturbed.

"Am I deaf?" Ey heard eir voice. There was no shuffle of sand as ey got to eir feet. Ey kicked at the water. Silence. Ey snapped next to both ears. Nothing. Ey looked back to the towel. Everything outside eir helmet was muted.

A pit grew in eir stomach.

Was the creature really gone? How much of this was real in the first place and how much a manipulation? Something very, very real had torn apart the panther-dog, but the towel had em questioning the reliability of eir senses. The air felt thick and close, but that towel never stopped moving.

Navigating only by the outlines of shadows, Maude surveyed the beach. Cliffside to eir left, ripples marking the sea to eir right. It was hard to tell where the sand ended and the ocean began. Ey couldn't look at anything directly, only out of the corner of eir eye, as if ey still had spots from the sun. The panther-dog looked small now, far away and marked only by the low shadow its body cast. Maude's throat tightened and ey looked away. Ey couldn't save anything.

Ey walked over to a strange shadow at eir feet and gave it a light kick. Driftwood. It must have been what tripped em. Ey spun in a slow circle, eyes flicking to check for other shadows on the beach. Whatever the creature was, it was huge. It wouldn't be easy for it to hide.

As ey stepped forward, the heavy feeling of being watched crept over em. The creature's presence swelled at eir back, but no shadow spread before em. As ey turned around the ringing picked up again, dimmer now with eir helmet on.

Maude faced the creature.

It cast no shadow, nothing to indicate it was visible at all, but ey felt its rippling energy radiating toward em, outmatched in strength only by the sun. Fear spiked in eir chest. Ey tried to move eir feet, but ey were frozen, muscles locked up in terror.

"I-I'm not mad, alright?" Maude said. "About the panther-dog, I mean."

The beast didn't move. Maude swallowed.

"I mean," ey continued, "I'm upset about it, but I get it. That's just the nature of nature, right? Things kill *other* things." *Maude* killed other things. Eaglets and panthers and innocent creatures.

Blood dripped from eir nose and onto eir lips. Maude licked at the salt it left.

"But you don't have to kill *me*," ey added hastily. "Oh." The realization struck em. "This is your home, isn't it?"

Ey thought about the cave at the far end of the beach and of the alcove at the back where the panther-dog had hid. The thought of it going further, of twisting deep down into the earth and out of sight, rose in eir mind.

"You must only come out in the hot weather when it's empty, huh?" Maude asked. "Probably not used to being disturbed."

The beast didn't react.

"In all the times I've been here, I've never once seen you…" Maude said quietly. "Well, I'm sorry for bothering you. I didn't know this was your home and I promise I won't come back if you let me go." A thin argument, but it was all ey could do.

There was one other option. The thin blade at the small of Maude's back burned like a second sun, out of sight but never far from Maude's mind.

The creature's ringing song escalated—ey hadn't realized it had started to taper—and its pressure pulsed in a powerful shove that forced Maude onto eir back. Eir breath grew ragged as the air thickened, about to burst. The creature hung over em once more. Pressure and anticipation gathered on eir chest like the thing rested on it. Ey struggled to breathe—to move, to run—but ey were pinned.

Maude wedged a hand underneath emself and closed eir hand around the hilt of eir blade, a piece of guilt as long as eir finger.

Long enough.

If ey angled it right.

The creature's breath fogged eir visor. Ey knew where its throat was.

Ey thought of deadweight wings and ringing silence. Ey thought of the feathers left behind, stuck in between wires on the fence, little ones clinging to Maude's clothes. Ey thought of crusted blood in eir fingernails, on the collar of a shirt ey never wore again.

Eir fingers tightened and ey burst into tears. Ey weren't ready to die. Ey didn't want to go alone like this, torn up and bleeding into the sand like the panther-dog. Like the eaglet.

Maude wondered who would find eir body first, if it would be a ranger sent after em when ey never returned, or if ey would rest there until the summer came. With the sun so strong, no one would be able to retrieve em until autumn. Eir body would bake under the sun for the whole season until eir blood dried and eir skin cracked.

Or the thing would just eat em. Turn Maude into life instead of death. Keep another kill from Maude's conscience.

Maude let go.

Eir fingers loosened and eir body went lax. Ey couldn't pick feathers out of a wire fence again. Were ey really worth more than the fox-eagle? Better to die by this creature than to take another life. Ey couldn't clean up another death.

Maude closed eir eyes and let the pressure engulf em. Ey imagined a weighted blanket, a body against eirs, comforting and safe. The beast would feast tonight on two lost creatures. Maybe the fox-eaglet would forgive Maude, if ey met it later. Maybe it would understand. It wanted to kill Maude too, once.

The presence of the beast expanded and forced down on Maude's chest until a rib cracked. Ey sobbed and braced for more. The wreckage ey would leave behind flashed with the white spots behind eir eyes, a perfect match to the fox-eaglet. To the panther-dog. Ey thought of the velvet fur on its nose and wished the creature was there now to purr and rumble for em.

And then it stopped.

The unnatural heat of the creature dissipated and its heavy, buzzing energy subsided.

Maude sat up gingerly and looked around. For all ey could tell, the beach lay empty. Even the corpse of the panther-dog was gone, the sand beneath it swept clean. In the distance the towel snapped, its sound once more audible through Maude's helmet.

With shaking hands, ey reached up to remove eir helmet. Ey closed eir eyes and slid it off one inch at a time. When ey were finally free, ey clutched eir helmet tight to eir chest and took a shuddering breath.

Waves lapped behind em and a stone tumbled from the cliffs. A light breeze brushed across eir face, so gentle it brought on another sob, this one sticky with snot and blood. Maude choked on a moan and leaned forward until eir forehead touched the sand.

The creature was gone.

Ey laid on eir stomach and cried.

When the tears cleared and steady breath returned, Maude scooted down toward the ocean. Ey traded eir own salt for the sea's and washed eir face clean. The sun didn't set on this forsaken planet and Maude had no gauge to tell how much time had passed. Ey walked to where the panther-dog had lain. A ring of blood remained, a bloom of moist gray against white.

Maude pulled eir blade from its sheath and dropped it into the sand. It landed hilt up, asking to be held once more, but Maude left it to be claimed by the tide.

Attack of the Dead Men

by
Charles Reis

Once the gas dissipated, seven thousand Imperial German troops advanced towards Osowiec Fortress, a dark blue wave that oozed over the blackened land. Erich remained with his battalion at the front. He grinned and kept a loose grip on his Mauser Gewehr 98 bolt-action rifle.

The young soldier surveyed the ravaged land through his gas mask. The sun glared down on the few trees that weren't cut down, their leaves yellowed and curled. A half mile away, trenches and foxholes circled the area. A thick forest lined the horizon beyond that. The fortress rested in the center of it all, exposed and vulnerable.

He maneuvered around tree stumps and walked past the dead birds that littered the damp ground. His mid-calf leather jackboots crushed the black grass. Smoking craters joined the scorched tanks and jeeps, monuments to the past brutal battles. He admired the handiwork of Field Marshal Paul von Hindenburg, who had earlier ordered the base's bombardment with bromine and chlorine gas.

Months of laying siege had finally paid off with a victory that made him want to cheer for their impending conquest. This was his first major battle, so Erich hoped his actions brought honor to his papa. Erich's mother died after giving birth to him, so they only had each other. As he marched, he sidestepped past a lifeless, bloodied horse that lay in the mud. He pushed down the glint of tears that tried to form in his blue eyes. Poor creature. It was the one part of war that shook him as it reminded him of how he and his papa bonded over their love of horses.

Since he was eight, they had frequently gone horseback riding on the family estate outside of Koblenz. Diamant, his father's prized black mare, was still stabled there. His father was a top general in the Imperial Army, and Erich fondly remembered the times his papa rode Diamant in military ceremonies. Before heading off for the war effort, his father left the care of Diamant in his only child's hands and told him that he couldn't have asked for a better son. His papa was shot dead while riding a horse during the invasion of Belgium back in August of 1914. A few months after his father's death, Erich turned seventeen and was conscripted into the Army. Erich glanced at the sky and imagined that his father smiled down on him from heaven.

Since his battalion led the way, Erich had a front-row view of the structure. The defensive walls showcased bullet holes, shattered bricks, and charred stones. The three dark gray onion domes of the church reached up from behind the walls. He smirked at the thought that Russians might have crawled into its sanctuary to pray for deliverance.

The metal gates of the Russian fortress creaked open. The Germans held their position two meters from the structure. The fact that anyone survived the attack gave Erich newfound respect for his enemy. He put his finger on the trigger and clamped his other hand on the wood forestock. Although he expected the Russians to surrender, he was also prepared for a fight.

About a hundred ghoulish Russians sprinted through the gate armed with rifles and attached bayonets. Erich sucked in a breath and took a step back. The Russians growled like a pack of wolves. Their pale skin blistered and peeled, and blood splattered their green uniforms. Red goo dripped from their ears and several had a gory mash of flesh where eyes once were. Some had bloodied white cloths wrapped around their mouths and noses. Though many limped, they ran faster than normal men. They coughed while they charged.

For a moment, Erich forgot how to breathe. His compatriots screamed and fled. They dropped their guns and trampled others, but he remained motionless. His muscles tightened. His commander yelled at them to hold the line, but no one listened.

"*Yehst! Yehst!*" one Russian screeched in a raspy voice. The other ghouls hissed and roared.

Erich's knuckles ached from gripping his weapon. The hair bristled on his neck. He had learned some Russian from his time on the Eastern Front. Hearing the enemy yell *Eat! Eat!* provoked his survival instinct. He tore off his mask and dropped his rifle. His body raged with adrenaline from running. Erich had witnessed comrades lose limbs and their lives from landmines, but he'd never seen anything so nightmarish as this. He had to escape from whatever disease the enemy had.

The artillery guns opened fire from the fortress. Screams and growls resonated through the air. Several Germans were gunned down. A few meters away, a Russian with an open wound for a nose pounced on a soldier. They fell to the ground and the Russian bit the man in the neck.

Erich sprinted towards a wrecked Austin-Kégresse car, a half-track armored fighting vehicle. Sweat poured down his face. A bullet whizzed by his ear. He crouched down by the vehicle's continuous track. The clangor of the bullets ricocheting off the metal pelted his ears. He stifled his breath and remained hidden.

Cries for help came from his left. Staying low, Erich peeked around the corner. A few meters away, a German soldier dug his fingers into the ground and crawled on his belly. Blood soaked his back. Three growling Russians surrounded him. They dropped their guns and dove for the man, digging into him like ravening beasts. Erich's pulse pounded in his eyes. He covered his mouth to stifle his gagging.

A ghoul with a beard chomped into the soldier's neck and his victim unleashed an ungodly scream. The Russian lifted his head with a large piece of flesh dangling from his mouth. With a grin on his face, he chewed it. The glutton used his fingers to push more of the flesh into his maw, teeth gnashing like a cow chewing its cud.

The German's arms twitched as blood squirted from the gash. Finally, he went silent. His head flopped to the ground. The other two ripped the man's body, tore off skin, and pulled out organs. Bones cracked as they snapped the limbs. Each bite they took pleased them. A Russian missing his eyes stopped to cough. Red sludge ejected from his mouth.

This was beyond the normal violence of war. Erich's stomach soured. His skin crawled. How can they eat a man alive? They weren't human, but they can't be monsters. Monsters didn't exist, Papa used to tell him. He darted toward the distant tree line that rested in the south. Amid the bullets and screams he quickened his pace. His feet kicked up dirt. He ran for many meters without stopping.

A massive barbed wire entanglement lay before him. He pushed his legs harder with a surge of determined energy. As he drew closer, the keen screech of a horse jabbed his eardrums. He wondered if a horse was dying, soon to become a crow-picked corpse like the one he saw earlier. He searched the battlefield and spotted a trapped black horse with wire wrapped around its front legs. It looked like a Mecklenburger with its long tapered neck, powerful legs, and deep chest and shoulders. The same breed as Diamant.

The horse jumped and kicked, but the wire grew tighter, tearing the skin and drenching its hair with blood. Its rider was stretched over an X-shaped post with wire coiled around his gore-drenched body. The man's blood pooled in the mud beneath his dangling head and arms.

A narrow path through the barbed wire maze led to safety. The horse's wailing drew him in, but he pulled away. He refused to look at the animal and focused ahead, but his heart demanded he help. An image burned through his mind of his father smiling while riding Diamant in a military procession. He pushed back his fears and raced to the animal. There won't be another dead horse.

Erich avoided the horse's back end as it kicked its hind legs hard enough to shatter a man's ribs. He grabbed the reins of the bridle and pulled, urging it to stay calm. The animal thrashed about. Erich pleaded while he caressed the horse's forehead, and the beast calmed as he gazed into its magnificent chestnut-colored eyes.

He didn't care about the danger—he had to save this animal. There were no Russians in sight. He retrieved a combat knife from his belt and sawed through the wires. He blocked out the explosions, screams, and the swaying corpse as he worked. His patient remained silent and still as rapid breathing expanded and contracted its body. Little by little, Erich unraveled then removed the pieces. Horse blood coated his gloved hands.

Time seemed to slow down. The slaughter raged around him, but he worked without flinching. When he freed the horse from the last wire, he slapped the sweat off his face and stood up. The animal held steady. Erich put his foot on the stirrup and prepared to mount.

A Russian jumped on him with a growl. Erich crashed onto his back and his knife fell out of his hand. The horse whinnied and galloped away, shrinking into the wasteland. The ghoul straddled him and Erich pressed his hands against the Russian's chest. His jaw clenched and sweat beaded down his face as he strained against his enemy.

The Russian's teeth clicked as he dug his nails into Erich's cheeks. Despite Erich's efforts, the man pushed harder, snapping like a crazed dog. Closer and closer, centimeter by centimeter, his teeth prepared to mangle.

The ghoul jerked back and coughed. Blood and tissue spewed from his mouth with each hack. The gore splattered over Erich's face and blond hair. He wailed. A pungent odor of rotting meat filled his nostrils, choking him. Although exhausted, the will to survive rallied his stamina. He spotted his knife a few centimeters away, reached with his quivering hand, and grabbed it. The man heaved, wracked with coughs. Erich held his breath and plunged the weapon into the ghoul's heart.

The Russian squealed and blood saturated his uniform. He ground his teeth. His red eyes fixed on Erich before he let out a gasp and collapsed to the side like a toppling tree.

The body twitched for several seconds, then stilled. The corpse's skin blistered and peeled in rapid decay.

Erich shoved the rest of the body off of him. He took several deep breaths to fight his exhaustion, laying in the mud as the music of war raged on. Fear spread through his body and stabbed his gut. He vaulted off the ground. He had to get out of here before more of those things found him.

He ran. He stomped through a mixture of mud and blood as he tore along the trenches. Erich glanced back to see if others pursued him. The sight of the dead Russian sitting up and yanking the knife from his chest washed away any bravery that remained.

Erich sprinted for the forest, still many meters away, pretending it led to salvation. He dodged the entanglements dotted over the land. Seconds felt like minutes as he rushed across the blasted battlefield. He jumped over a corpse. His boots slid on entrails and he fell into a foxhole. Mud splashed over him. He lay there, breathing heavily.

He cried out, *"Papa!"* He hadn't done that since childhood when he had frequent nightmares about *Der Schwarze Mann*, a boogeyman that tried to eat him. When he called, his father always came to comfort his son instead of sending the hired help. Papa told him never to be afraid since monsters don't exist. Erich needed his papa there to tell him that the monsters he saw weren't real.

He considered his father brave, but was he on the day he died? Did he cry out for his papa as he bled out in a pile of mud and shit? Maybe the bleeding and the pain grew so intense that he cursed the country that sent him there. The ghouls might have sent such a wave of terror through him that he would have cried like a child. Maybe he became a ghoul until something finished him off.

One thing Erich did know: his father would want him to survive.

He pushed himself off the ground and climbed up the slope of the foxhole. He slid down from the blood and urine-drenched mud, but he thrust his body to the top. He sprinted. The wailing of a man and the growls of the ghouls echoed from behind. The *thunk thunk thunk* of the guns hammered over it all. He tried to block it out, but it haunted him.

"*Papa!*" Saliva surged into his throat.

"*Papa!*" His breaths short and broken.

"*Papa!*" Shock and terror overtook his brain like a flood, washing his memory of the rest of that day.

* * *

A week after the battle, Erich appeared in Berlin before representatives of Erich von Falkenhayn, chief of the German General Staff. For several hours he gave his testimony. The entire time his body fidgeted and his legs bounced while he sat in a chair. He gave a detailed report of the battle, but particularly focused on the Russian rising despite the knife in his heart.

The representatives dismissed his testimony, along with that of the other survivors. They concluded that the shock of witnessing the effects of the gas attack caused the German troops to panic. Some officials suggested the Germans might have breathed some of the gas themselves, resulting in hallucinations. The Russians were dying, but they weren't undead.

Erich never accepted that conclusion. With the fortress destroyed by the Russian Army, there was no way to prove what really happened on August 6, 1915. Time didn't heal his damaged mind. Even months after the end of the Great War, the horrors he witnessed still plagued his dreams.

On a chilly March afternoon, Erich, sporting a week's worth of facial growth, leaned back into his dining chair. Sunlight glared through the large windows, exposing the thick dust that shrouded the green curtains and wood floors of the cold room. The *tick-tocks* from the grandfather clock was the only sound accompanying him.

He didn't know how long he sat there, nor did it matter. His hand rested on the table, gripping a near-empty glass of whiskey. Near his knuckles stood a tall half-empty bottle. He grabbed it and filled his glass up to the brim. Whiskey in the morning, in the afternoon, and in the evening. Much like most men that came back from the war, Erich's new companion had become the drink.

He gulped the alcohol, then he glanced over at the Luger pistol laying on the table. He kept it with him for protection due to the rise in crime. Sometimes, he placed the short barrel in his mouth or on his temple. Each time he held the gun in place longer and longer. When he did, his mind flashed with images of the Russians. He contemplated whether to pull the trigger.

He stood, grabbed the pistol, and placed it in the holster. He already had the gun in his mouth this morning, and he didn't need to do it again. He downed the whiskey, slammed the glass on the table, then adjusted his long coat. It was time for him to be with his horses, the only thing that gave him any happiness.

The wood creaked as he opened the barn door. When he stepped into the structure, he inhaled the aroma of hay. To some the smell was revolting, but to Erich, it brought calm that glowed in his heart. His papa felt the same way. Horse grunts and snorts played out, but with less than a third of the thirty stables occupied, it wasn't what Erich was used to before the war. His family's farm had a large drop in income due to Germany's diminishing wealthy elite, resulting in fewer people housing their horses here. Despite that, Erich worked on his farm to seek solitude after leaving the army.

He went to the first horse to his left, a black mare. Like he had done many times over the past several months, he reached into his pocket for an apple and held up the fruit.

"*Guten Morgen,* Diamant."

The horse bit down on the apple, taking it from Erich's hand. He caressed Diamant's head, then kissed her on the snout. Pleasant memories of his father riding his mare around the farm or on the nearby blooming meadows soothed his mind.

With Diamant chewing her treat, Erich walked to the opposite stall toward a black stallion.

"*Guten Morgen,* Phönix."

He retrieved another apple and fed it to the horse. When he discovered the horse he saved survived the battle with only scars on its legs, he requested to keep the animal. Since his father was highly respected throughout the country, the army allowed it. He named him Phönix, since the horse rose from the ashes of war. Erich stroked the horse's mane.

A prickling sensation like insects crawled over his skin as he glanced at the empty stable next to Phönix. A large, distinct shadow, darker than coal, enveloped the far corner.

It devoured all light near it. From this strange mass glowed red eyes, blazing like flames in a lantern. He had seen it before; his body wanted to run, but he remained in place. Saliva swelled in his mouth and sweat formed on his face. His vision warped and bent.

The shadow weaved into the shape of a man. As if it emerged from hell, the unknown figure formed into a familiar sight: The Russian ghoul he stabbed years ago. The eyes blazed brighter and the discolored skin of purple, blue, and red peeled off its gruesome face. Erich's knife remained plunged in the monster's chest. Behind him, the horses whickered and snorted softly, unconcerned with the accursed thing that came to haunt him.

"*Yehst! Yehst!*" The Russian drew closer.

Erich gasped for breath, throat tight. A prickling sensation overwhelmed his quivering body. He wanted to look away, but his eyes locked on the macabre vision. With each step he took, the ghoul snapped his jaws and hissed.

Closer and closer the Russian came, bringing back memories of the battle. Erich squeezed his eyes shut in horror and nausea and pressed his forehead against the horse's snout.

He'd experienced this all before and he knew he would experience it again.

"*Papa.*" The passage of time had not healed his trauma.

"*Papa.*" His heart rumbled in his chest.

"*Papa.*" He needed his father to tell him that monsters don't exist.

He felt the horsehair over his hot skin. He took several deep and controlled breaths. With each one, his senses gradually returned to their former state. It took a few minutes for the dread to reduce to a tolerable level. Once it did, he opened his eyes.

The monster jumped on him. Erich crashed onto his back. He screamed; the horses wailed and bumped into their stalls. The ghoul straddled him. Erich clenched his jaw and pressed his hands against the Russian's chest. This couldn't be real! These visions vanished after he calmed down. Not today. He called for help but doubted anyone was there to hear him.

The Russian hissed and pressed his nails into Erich's cheeks. The enemy crept in closer, snapping his jaw. He prepared to rip the flesh off his prey. The ghoul coughed, spewing blood and tissue from his mouth. It splattered over Erich's face. He grabbed his pistol and aimed for the Russian's head.

The ghoul was gone. Erich jumped off the hay covered ground. He held the gun out, spun around, and glanced around the barn. No blood. No ghoul. Just him and the horses. These visions plagued his dreams, but sometimes they haunted him when awake. This hallucination had been the worst. If his father was there with him now, he would hug his son.

A burst of raspy laughter spewed from behind. Erich jerked around. His eyes bulged at the sight of the Russian. The smiling man stood near the stall and exposed his pinkish teeth. He pulled the knife from his chest. Blood squirted from the wound and dripped onto the uniform and the ground. The ghoul waved the knife around like a tree branch dancing in the wind. Gore spewed from his mouth.

He gripped the pistol tight and fired. Three bullets aimed for the Russian, but like smoke in the wind, the ghoul vanished. The horses wailed and weaved side to side in their stalls. A few reared their legs. Erich didn't see the horse in the stall where the bullets entered but heard the cries.

"Diamant?" Erich said in a shaky voice. He rushed over and pulled the stable door open.

A wave of sorrow broke through Erich's soul. He couldn't breathe. His stomach fluttered. His heart throbbed. His muscles stiffened. Papa's horse lay on her side. He thought of the dead horse at the battle.

Diamant bobbed her head. Drool fell from her mouth. She bit at the top of her front leg where the wound resided.

Erich rushed over and dropped to his knees. The pistol fell to his side. Tears poured down his cheeks as he caressed the horse's head. The wound was deep, and Erich feared it may have hit a bone. He pressed down on it and felt the warm blood against his skin. He placed his forehead on the horse's stomach. Her cries echoed in his ears. His body trembled. What had he become? How could he have shot Diamant? Would his father hate him?

He remained there. That battle was four years ago. Four years of dread. Four years of torment. Four years of trauma. He tried to beat back what haunted him with whiskey and his horses. Instead, it got harder to tell what was real and what was fake. His precious Diamant, the connection to his father, was on the ground from his own hands.

The horse rubbed her snout and head against Erich's back. The man shook his head and squeezed his eyes. Of course Diamant forgave him, he thought, since the horse was part of his family. Erich eyed the pistol. There were plenty of bullets left.

His next move left him pondering. What haunted him was getting worse, and no doubt it would overtake his sanity. His continued breakdown was now evident in his crime against Diamant. Maybe there was no hope, and he should end it himself. The horse's injury may have shattered the bones in the leg. Those types of injuries usually resulted in the horse being put down. Could he do that? Maybe he could try to heal her up?

Much like what happened to his country, which suffered from inflation, unemployment, and a humiliating defeat, he had become sad and broken. Erich took the gun. He stroked the horse and leaned his head against her own. His knuckles ached from the grip. He remained there and thought about his father. He hoped his father would understand. They both went through hell, but his papa was lucky enough to die on the battlefield. Erich wished he had too.

He loved his father deeply, but the man did lie. Monsters do exist.

The Cuff

by
Lauren Starnino

"You know the difference between a weed dealer and an H dealer?"

"What is it?"

"Weed dealers don't have customers. They only have friends."

Matteo tried but wasn't able to muster up a giggle, let alone a laugh. He was too uncomfortable. Too tense. Too anxious. That's the main problem with being a socially awkward person, you never get used to the feeling of said awkwardness. Matteo never felt at home in his own skin. He never felt in command of the space he occupied. A cruel and bitter battle-axe of a guidance counselor once told him he was *ineffectuality personified.* Matteo had never heard the word ineffectuality, and although it sounded like muddled English, there it was in the dictionary. He was pretty offended when he read the entry. His guidance counselor, a real tragedy of a human being, also said anywhere he went he would be out of place. What could you do?

Matteo's high school years fell in the eighties, when America was kicking political correctness in the ass of its acid wash jeans. Most of Matteo's teachers called him Matt, even after he timidly tried to correct them. It was the norm for people to speak unfiltered in those days, so who worried about improperly nicknaming a student and slighting a person's Italian ethnicity in one swift motion? Matt was much easier for Matteo's ignorant teachers to pronounce.

"Is that a joke? Are you making some kind of point?" Matteo asked. Judging by his level of dope sick discomfort, he had to have been walking for about forty minutes, ten with his new buddy beside him. Forty minutes of meandering around the grimiest dope haunts he knew. His phone was turned off and he didn't have cash for gas. He had seven singles and nothing else, which basically meant no money at his disposal. At his most desperate, he had shamelessly begged for five dollars' worth of H to no avail.

Matteo's plan today was to hang out in the Olneyville area of Providence in hopes of finding a new source.

And ripping them off.

Matteo had not shared that part of his plan with his new walking buddy. Drake, Matteo's new pal, was under the impression that they were pooling their cash to buy a twenty-dollar bag. Matteo had never heard of a twenty-dollar bag, but all dealers had their own style.

"I'm trying to be a better conversationalist," Drake answered flatly.

Drake walked a bit ahead of Matteo. It would be doing him a favor to say he was thin or lean. Drake was gaunt. Pointy and sharp where the human body was meant to have the softness of flesh. He was all black body hair and lank in a faded maroon hoodie. It hung on him like these sad curtains Matteo remembered from his nonna's house. His footsteps were slight and fast. As Drake continued on ahead, Matteo found himself zoning out on Drake's spindly shadow cast by the blazing July morning sun.

The street shot through a cluster of abandoned mills. Matteo took in the massive brick buildings, lined with rows upon rows of cloudy glass windows. It seemed every other pane was cracked or broken, and what remained looked like ancient rusty knives stabbing in all different directions. He tried to imagine this area of Providence a hundred years ago: a complex nucleus of machinery and steel and fumes, a hub of industrial era mechanisms all manned by the working class of the day. Now the factories stood vacant.

Matteo thought back to history classes in school—those he sat in as a student, then later went on to teach. As a student and teacher he looked forward to covering the Industrial Age in America. Matteo had not taught for nearly eighteen months now. His days no longer began at 7 a.m. with a shower, shave, and triple espresso. Nine Inch Nails, Rage Against the Machine, and Wu-Tang Clan routinely scored his duck and weave through I-95's morning rush hour traffic. Now his days began four to six hours after he last used. Every morning his eyes blinked open to the droning sound of the TV and the feeling of a thousand centipedes racing under his skin, biting and itching, tiny legs poking at every nerve.

He grew edgier with every step. The soles of his sneakers were bald, as smooth as a marble, and the impact of the concrete felt like mallets pounding into his heels. The farther they walked, the higher the ache spread up his legs. The withdrawal was setting in, and he knew it wouldn't be long before this dull ache radiated throughout his entire body. A furious roar of unrelenting pain was just around the corner.

"Are we close or what…? I feel like absolute dog shit, my friend." Matteo forgot Drake's name, but he had to ask how much longer this jaunt was going to be.

"Not to worry, chief. The building we want is on the next block," Drake answered while shuffling along. He wore oversized black jeans, worn and ripped at the bottom from dragging across the ground.

Drake was depressing to look at. But right then, everything seemed pretty bleak. Moments between picking up and using—that is to say, life—was just a sad scene. This was the classic scenario that lit this notion in flashing neon. Flat broke, sick as a flea bitten and starved stray dog, depressed and desperate. However, he did manage a soft smirk when it occurred to him that the skin and bones in a maroon hoodie had likely forgotten his name too. A stranger becoming your right-hand man in an instant was a common thing in the addict lifestyle. It was all about making connections and networking while having the cunning street smarts for spotting the ones just running around looking for someone to rip off. You had to choose your running partner very carefully. Which, much to Matteo's satisfaction, his new beanpole buddy had failed to do.

Matteo's pulse quickened while he recapped his strategy to successfully burn this dude. This was a monumental risk, but when facing the all-consuming big W's, it was one thousand percent justified.

His plan was the following: accompany his new wiry buddy (Drake? Derek?) to meet the connect, and insist on going with Drake/Derek (or David?) because in the past he had been burned—people had taken his cash and ran, leaving him broke and sick. This was the dodgy part, the glimmering razor's edge upon which the whole situation balanced. At the actual hand off, Matteo had to spontaneously figure a way to get ahold of the bag and run. This was the difficult part of a scam. The totally unpredictable and unplannable part. If he could get ahold of the bag without triggering any metaphoric alarms and tipping them off that they're about to get stiffed, he'd be shot out of a cannon by a blast of adrenaline and the running off part was effortless.

Drake perked up. "Here it is, chief. This place looks wicked spooky, I swear."

Matteo stared at the building. It loomed over him in a quiet stillness that made him feel like he was being watched right back.

"He's inside this place? Who deals out of an abandoned factory? I've heard about cops checking on spots like this." The unexpected development rattled him. Now he would have to navigate the interior of an unfamiliar place. Scanning the surroundings of the structure, he noted a long line of parked cars in the nearby empty lot. Rows and rows of luxury vehicles glinting under the sun: Bentleys, Maseratis, Cadillacs, and Porsches, and he swore he could see the nose of a white Lamborghini.

"Nah, no cops around here. Storage spaces inside, and some artist spaces too, I think. But mostly vacant." Drake pointed up to the second level at an illuminated block of windows.

Matteo took in the exterior of the factory. Rows and columns of cloudy, rusty panes with nothing but black behind them, except for one block of four windows lit up in hazy orange-yellow. He knew this was the last good opportunity to hit the eject button on his plan. A ball of fire rose in his chest, and the overwhelming sense of the unknown wreaked havoc on his mind and body.

A thought rose above the din of anxious chatter in his mind. Why hadn't Drake asked to see Matteo's cash? Most people will ask right out of the gate—it's one of the easiest and most common precautions to take.

A warm nausea churned in his gut. Stomach acid seethed and rose up his throat like waves crashing and foaming at the shore. Matteo ignored his mental static and followed Drake through the double doors made of iron, blood red and shrieking from its scabs of rust. There's a fail-safe adage known to all addicts, whether they're rookies or seasoned vets. He mustered up the confidence to press on by exclaiming in his mind two little words: fuck it.

As the doors fell shut and muted the morning sunlight from outside, the scuffle of rushed footsteps scurried by on the sidewalk where Matteo had stood only moments ago. A quote from one of Matteo's favorite books, *The Art of War* by Sun Tzu, flashed in his brain like a pop-up ad. *Startled beasts indicate that a sudden attack is coming.*

An ancient elevator huffed and puffed them to the second level. Drake stood statue still until his beeping phone snapped him to movement. He lifted his cell and pressed answer with the single pinky finger on his right hand. The other digits were missing to the knuckle so only a scarred, blunted stump of a palm remained. When their gazes met, Drake flashed a wide and sly smile, all crooked teeth and narrowed eyes.

Drake answered, "Coming up plus one."

Matteo wondered why he didn't call this person during their walk to let him know they were on their way to meet him. He hadn't heard that lingo used before, and surprises were not welcome. But, to be fair, plugs and connects could be finicky types.

"I didn't realize you had a phone. He knows we're coming?" Matteo asked.

Drake only grunted in response.

The elevator nudged to a stop and the door slid open. They stepped out into a wide-open space, punctuated by banks of machines. The layout reminded Matteo of a cubicle farm you would see in a modern-day call center, only the ceiling had to be fifty feet high. A loft of wood wide enough to comfortably walk across lined the perimeter, and the din of lively conversations and laughing filled the room. Underneath the cheerful voices music played, something bubblegum and upbeat. Hanson's "MMMBop" fluttered out of speakers unseen.

A man lunged from hiding against the wall and grabbed Matteo around the arm. Matteo yanked against his hold with a startled cry, but then a second man was on him, wrenching his other arm down.

"Stand still and don't speak," the first man said.

"What the fuck is going on?! Let me go!"

Matteo thrashed between them. His bald sneakers slid on the concrete as they muscled his arms down with brute strength and held him still. He felt outside of his body. A stranger in his own skin. He searched around the room.

People lined the loft around the perimeter of the space. Whether they were men or women, old or young, he couldn't tell. Every figure above wore a black shroud from head to toe. Their faces were obscured by thin veils that mostly resembled the nude color of panty hose you see in drug stores.

"Let me out of here!"

The spectators stood silent and unmoved.

Matteo's gut dropped. That's what they were, spectators. He was the show.

"Stop it." One of the men spun Matteo so the two of them stood face to face. He was all bulk under a burlap apron, arms and legs like tree trunks, his medicine ball of a head covered in a ski mask. Gold teeth glinted as he spoke. "Now shut up, look, and listen. If you don't retain the following instructions you'll lose your chance and the next one will be brought in."

Lose what chance?

A light in the center of the room flicked on—that same hazy, yellow-orange light from the windows. The beam shone on a massive machine. Pale green plates of metal encased the majority of the structure, and the moving parts were stainless steel. It didn't look dull or obsolete. It looked efficient, operational.

Matteo didn't understand what a machine like this would be doing in a building of this age and condition. It powered on, hissed and rumbled to life. Rotating gears thrust steel arms, each the diameter of a baseball bat. The arms glided away from each other then closed together like a set of automatic doors at the supermarket, but never quite touched. The rhythm produced a deep hum.

A voice boomed from the loft above. "Now, my friends, let's show our new player what this machine is capable of! Most fortunate contender, I give you, The Cuff!"

The man on Matteo's right let him go and walked to the machine. He stood to the side and fed a thin metal bar into one of the machine's openings. The tree trunk of a man struggled a bit against the heft of the metal bar's weight until the machine caught the offering and pulled it in with a *chunk*.

"Watch the machine effortlessly cuff!" The announcer said.

From what Matteo discerned, the metal bar was fed into the machine, and in one seamless function the bar was cut and curled into a circle, then held in place to be joined with the next loop of metal. The bar was cuffed into joining links. When the clink of the metal hit the ground, he understood the finished product. The machine made chains.

Realizing only one man held him, Matteo thrashed and bucked his body weight with all the strength he could summon. Incoherent thoughts whizzed through his mind now. Fragmented words and memories blipped by from the spike of anxiety. Anyone who ever told Matteo that exercise helps ease withdrawal symptoms could die a long and slow death for saying so. Every cell in his body was screaming in his face, demanding to know why he was calling on his body and brain in such a way.

The man holding him was like stone, and twice his size. His bones ached in his captor's grip.

"Now, your chance to rival this mighty machine is upon you!"

A roar of cheers and applause thundered through the space. All conversations ceased. The glares from every figure above lasered onto Matteo. Servers wove through the spectators with cocktails and a mirrored platter exchanged hands. One of the voyeurs rolled their veil above their nose and leaned over the platter.

A pang of longing stabbed into his chest, and the pain sunk to his gut like a blade slitting a sheet from top to bottom.

The music rose and a new song blared on. It was "Don't Worry Be Happy" by Bobby McFerrin. Matteo felt like he was the subject of some perverse circus act.

"NO! Please, no! I don't want to do this! Just let me go, I won't tell anyone!" Matteo's voice echoed off the brick and rafters. At first he wasn't sure he was the one speaking. The hum of the machine, cheers of the audience, and Bobby McFerrin's crooning drowned out the desperate cries pouring out of him.

"Best of luck to our newest player!"

Gold Teeth shoved and nudged Matteo closer to the machine. The beat of his heart banged up his throat, and terror sharpened his senses. He glanced around the space seeking an escape, a savior, some kind of refuge.

Another hulk of a man stood at the far end of the room next to Drake's bony figure, arm extended to offer a baggie of powder. In a single motion Drake snatched the baggie with his good hand and buried it in his pocket, and then he jogged back the way they came in. As the elevator door closed Drake lifted his hood over his head, gaze locked on the ground. Just like that, Drake was gone.

Gold Teeth hauled Matteo before the machine where the two largest prongs met. Where the metal was cuffed. As he looked closer, he regained sensation in his otherwise terror-numbed body. Puddles of goopy, coagulated blood, fingers, partial ravages of hands, and small piles of skin, flesh, and bone filled the bottom of the machine. A cold sweat overcame him and his teeth chattered.

The gold-toothed man gave him a shake to garner his attention. "Here's what you have to do. Watch where the arms meet, and you'll see exactly what you came for being fed right into the opening between the arms. If you successfully grab the bag, you can leave. Try as many times as you want to snatch the little sucker. Keep your eyes on the gap between the arms." Words rattled out like boilerplate from a notary public.

Matteo tried to focus his gaze, but his vision was blurred with tears and the violent chattering of his teeth. It amazed him that, even in the midst of this outlandish nightmare, the withdrawals were mounting. The onslaught of terror, disbelief, and panic surged through him. His joints twitched and jerked. As he fought against his body's involuntary actions, he spotted the little baggies appearing between the machine's arms. The metal bar was no longer there. Now the prongs met the same as before, but instead of cuffing metal into a loop, they decimated the tiny bags of powder.

All at once someone hit mute on his racing thoughts and it clicked. He knew what was being fed into the machine, what was in the "gap between the arms" that Gold Teeth barked about. He knew what he had to do in order to leave this place. Second by second, thrust by thrust, the prongs squashed and destroyed the little bags. The powder was eviscerated into a substance so fine it floated away and disappeared before his eyes. Matteo took a deep breath, felt the hammering of his heart, and steadied himself.

To make a decent attempt at a grab, Matteo first blinked away the sweat and tears that stung his eyes. He steadied his breathing a notch by inhaling through his nose and exhaling out of his mouth. He let the exhales out as smooth as possible through the chatter of his teeth. It was wild what rose up through the chaos of panic-stricken thoughts; Matteo likened the vibrating of his jaws to an old television ad he loved when he was a kid where hundreds of tiny steel marbles on the surface of a massive subwoofer swirled and buzzed around from the output of sound. The mix of withdrawals and fear quieted to a dull roar.

He continued on, sneakers scuffing across the smooth concrete floor with the kind of baby steps one takes while waiting in a packed, creeping line of people. The roll and squish of something under his sneakers interrupted his gait. Matteo refused to react and look at the floor. He knew he was stepping on other people's fingers, first with a tender squish, then the hardness of the bone met his foot as he dropped his full weight.

"One grab. I'm making one, single grab and running back to the elevator," he whispered to himself. "If I can't do this in one try, I'm not letting this machine mangle my hands."

He stared into the tiny space between the machine's arms where the baggies appeared. Focused on the rhythmic open and close of the arms. Lifting his arm was like swimming to the surface of a pool with cinder blocks for feet.

"One grab. It'll take one second and then before you know it you'll be back outside."

He raised his arm, pointed his index, middle finger, and thumb, poised to pluck the little bag at the precise moment before the arms met and destroyed it.

A vivid image of the arms mashing his fingers to a pulp flashed and he flinched away from the gap. He had gotten maybe two or three inches away from the movement of the machine and by pure instinct, his arm jerked away. Like some horrific game of slaps he played with his friends in the schoolyard, his hand flew back as if someone else yanked it.

A booming voice from above said, "This is not a task for menial bench hands! Only the highest skilled workers are a match for this marvel of industry!"

Underneath the proud voice came excited gasps and menacing cheers.

He steeled himself. Puffed his chest out, flexed his biceps and balled his fists. He was more determined than ever.

"You psycho fucks!" The fear and panic boiled down to simple rage. Rage at the weirdos in robes, at the machine, at his addiction, at himself.

"My esteemed guests, I think we have, as they say, a LIVE one!"

Thunderous cheers and maniacal roars of approval followed.

School teacher Matteo from eighteen months ago urged him to run. *If you don't quit now, you really do deserve to lose your hands.* School teacher Matteo and addict Matteo knew it was the smart thing to do. But no one guarded the elevator. The gold-toothed, ski-masked refrigerator stood at ease. No one would stop him if he decided to flee.

The drug-seeking brain can be an indelible force, a brick plunked down on the gas pedal of a Mack truck barreling towards the edge of a cliff.

Expectations reset and reluctance brushed off. Okay, it looked like this wasn't a one and done situation. Matteo equated the challenge facing him with any other hoop an addict must jump through to pick up: arriving at three locations and waiting at each one just to be told to head to another, leaving nagging voicemails and texts while the mounting frustration made him want to rip his hair out, arguing with weasel pawn brokers over the value of a gold charm his nana and papa gave him decades ago for his First Communion. If he still had that charm today he'd grasp it for luck, but it was pawned and never recovered.

The thumb, middle, and index finger pluck attempt was a fail. Doing his best to memorize the machine's rhythm, he again forced his right arm to lift. He focused in on the tiny gap, a space that was no thicker than the width of his thumbnail. The entire universe could be sucked into a black hole and all he knew was this scintilla of a mark. Eons passed as he closed the last centimeter between his fingertips and the baggie. He blinked and what came next was a vicious attack on the right side of his upper body.

The Cuff devoured the cuff of his sleeve, then sucked in and ground on his fingers. Blood bloomed through the tan fabric. He planted his feet as firmly as he could amidst the fallen and rotting hands, fingers, and nails, all chewed and spit out by the machine, grabbed onto his wrist, and tugged.

With the first yank the pain morphed into an atom bomb explosion of agony. When he was twelve, he lit a firecracker in his hand and tossed it the instant the flame ran out of fuse. He remembered thinking his entire hand was blown to shreds by the level of pain it created. Matteo suspected this is how he'd have felt if he were holding five hundred firecrackers that day.

A crescendo of cheers hit him like a bucket of ice water. Then the triumphant voice: "Ladies and gentleman, we have a ROBUST contender in our midst!"

The blaring white light of pain faded, clearing his vision. The machine tugged his entire shirt now. The neckline stretched over his right shoulder. A stinging numbness was all he felt in his wrist and hand. Every other part of his body was screaming.

The machine continued to operate as if nothing had changed. It was an unstoppable force. A rhythmic muscle made of steel, rumbling, clinking, humming away. Up close, Matteo could see the multitude of moving parts working behind the arms. Gears, shafts, blunted prongs, and, most lethally, smooth metal discs. It was these discs that tirelessly spun, dragging and pulling at his fingers and shirt.

It would take his arm.

The self-preservation instinct was also an unrelenting force. Matteo released his wrist, grabbed his shirt, pulled it over his head, and let the machine devour what it wanted. The shirt flew into the disc's grip and to everyone's utter shock, it hesitated and stuttered in its motion like a car about to stall out.

The baggies still appeared, sitting in the space and waiting to be grabbed or crushed. His shirt was dropping to the floor, thin shreds of tan fabric falling like streamers. *My shirt is ruined.* Another absurdly rational thought. He snatched at the open space between the arms and grabbed a fistful of baggies.

Some spectators gasped. Most were silently nonplussed. Matteo's leaps and strides toward the elevator were broken by the man with the tree trunk legs and ski mask. He blocked the entry to the elevator.

Tree Trunk crossed his tree limb arms and widened his shoulders.

A white robed figure crept closer and lifted his veil, revealing a clean-shaven, smiling face and perfectly whitened and capped teeth. His green eyes were wild with joy. "To the victor belong the spoils! Let us congratulate our brave challenger of The Cuff!" He took Matteo's hands in his. "My friend, return with fresh challengers and enjoy the fruits of your victory."

The veiled eyes from above burned into him. The next sound was the elevator car halting and the doors opening. Matteo jerked away, startled by the unexpected noise of another machine.

In one step he hopped on the elevator and collapsed to the floor. He heard cheering the entire ride down to the lower level before he stumbled into the bright light of day. He walked a block back the way he came and found a stoop to finally rest his body. Afraid to look, Matteo slowly removed his right hand from his jeans pocket. A breath he didn't realize he was holding escaped his lungs when he saw his fingers still there, coated with blood and swollen three times over. The flesh was so dark his fingers were blue and purple. He shoved his hand back in his pocket and tucked it in the lining as best as he could. He clutched four baggies in his left hand. All he could do was stare at them, feel the pain in his right hand, and cry.

One bag was spent. It quelled the pain and dimmed the sunlight to a mellow haze. He cried softly until he dozed off to sleep holding himself in his arms.

A light breeze spurred goosebumps on his skin and made the short hairs on his chest stiffen. He awoke to two big eyes staring into his. A girl of maybe eighteen blocked the sun and fiddled with a silver link chain around her neck. Her clothes were clean, expensive. The sapphire jewel on her gold class ring winked at him.

"…What's up?" He didn't know what else to say.

"Hangin' out. Waiting for my friends to meet up with me," she answered.

Her demeanor was far different from what he expected. She sounded confident, unafraid. Natural, even.

"Here? The mall is downtown." His right hand throbbed. He felt the ache in his teeth. Groggy and exhausted, he wasn't in the mood for a new friend.

"I need to pick up. For me and my boyfriend."

"No you don't."

"We're trying to get some painkillers. Or H. Whichever is fine." She spoke like he hadn't said a word.

Across the street a bus hissed to a stop and its doors folded open. Matteo jumped at the mechanical sounds. A man in his forties approached, sporting a five o' clock shadow with an unlit cigarette hanging out of his mouth, a Red Sox hat, and baggy clothes. It was the look of a person trying to seem younger. He walked halfway towards them and began a light jog once he spotted Matteo. Now a trio, Sox Hat joined them, placed an arm around the teenybopper, and planted a territorial kiss on her lips. She drew inward and looked at the ground. It was evident this girl was totally at home in her submissive role in their relationship.

Sox Hat lit his cigarette, looked at Matteo, and nodded hello. "You know where we can pick up? I got cash." He stared at him through the plume of smoke he exhaled.

In seconds his outstretched palm was padded with bills by the teenybopper. She closed her purse, glanced at Matteo's bloodstained pocket, then quickly returned her gaze to the ground.

Matteo stood slowly and motioned only to Sox Hat to follow him. The throb in his hand returned to full force.

"I know a place."

Kelly's Motto

by
Theresa Katin

Darkness spilled into town and settled like wet cement. Thick and slow, but once set it wouldn't be easy to get rid of. It nestled between houses and washed over streets, soaking them in twilight. Tree limbs rocked sluggishly in the wind as if dragged through ink. Small bursts of warm, pulsating yellow punctuated the dusk, the largest of which emanated from the house at 63 Begonia Drive.

Hauling a large, black garbage bag over her shoulder, Kelly Howell opened the door connecting the kitchen to the garage. The smell greeted her first, rolled over her in dank waves with notes of something sour. She stared into the pitch-black room and put both hands on the slippery bag. Her knees buckled and threatened to collapse under the weight, but she kept her balance.

The encroaching darkness receded as soon as Kelly flicked the light switch. One puny bulb dangled from the ceiling. Its meager glow pushed the twilight to the edges of the garage, illuminating the space like an angler fish. Kelly lugged the garbage bag to an open can and swung it inside. A rancid odor wafted from the trash can and stung her nostrils. She swatted away flies and slammed the lid shut.

Kelly was peeling off her yellow cleaning gloves when the phone rang. She didn't know anyone who would be calling at this hour, so she took her time getting to the living room.

She picked up the telephone. "Hello?"

A deep, gravelly voice filled the speaker and rolled into her ear.

"What a lovely night we're having."

Kelly frowned. "Who is this?" *Probably some stupid teenagers.*

"The moon shines whiter than bone and the breeze is colder than the breath of the dead. It's a perfect night for wearing lots of layers. Fleece, nylon, wool. Some would argue that the human skin is best for retaining warmth, and I don't disagree." The words oozed down Kelly's spine like tar.

"Who is this?" she repeated. These kids were getting way out of hand. Kelly sat on the living room couch, unbothered, and picked at a dark crust under her fingernails.

"Who am I? What a fascinating question. I have collected many names, but you might know me as—"

"Ooh, can I guess?" she interrupted. "Let me think…oh, wait. I don't care." Kelly hung up on the mystery caller.

She stood and returned to the kitchen when the phone rang again. Kelly ignored it and opened the cabinet under the kitchen sink. She pulled out a rag, a bucket, and a bottle of bleach, set them on the counter, and grabbed a new pair of yellow gloves. When she glanced at the window over the sink, she caught her reflection looking back. A dark stain from the leaky trash spread across the hem of her shirt.

The phone kept ringing. She filled the bucket with water, hoping the noise would drown out the ringtone, but the sound cut clean through. *I have so much to get done tonight. I do not have time for this.* Kelly groaned and picked up the phone again.

"What do you want?" she sighed.

"I want to talk to you. At least, I did. If you hadn't so rudely hung up on me earlier, we could've had a nice, intelligent conversation. But now I'm afraid the time for talking is over."

"Oh, you wanted an intelligent conversation? Well, if you were smart, you would leave me alone."

"Or what?"

She rolled her eyes. "I don't have time for this. I have urgent business to deal with."

"Oh, I'm so sorry my call is inconvenient for you. I just wanted to talk. But unfortunately, you've ruined that opportunity." The caller spoke slowly, enunciating every word as if they wanted to make sure Kelly understood them.

What Kelly understood was that she was pissed. Here she was, trying to have a productive evening, and this idiot was wasting her precious time.

"Look, buddy, if you want to play the serial killer game with me, you're wasting my time. Are you standing on my street? On my front lawn? Are you peering into my windows, looking at my things, piecing together my life? Trying to figure me out just so you can freak me out?" Kelly sat back down on the couch and crossed her legs. "Or, for a real twist, are you already inside? Is this some *When a Stranger Calls* type of thing? Whatever you're trying to do, it's not very creative. In fact, if you're not already inside, come on in! I don't do all this cleaning just for me. Don't be shy, now. Come in, take a look around. I have a lovely home."

A beeping noise came from the landline; the stranger had hung up. Kelly smirked. *Of course they hung up. Stupid*

She placed the phone on the coffee table and went back to the kitchen to collect her supplies. Outside, the wind picked up and rattled the trees viciously. It was almost one in the morning.

Kelly padded down the stairs to the basement. The stairs were covered in a dull brown carpet with flecks of green and orange, an odd combination that she always thought looked like cat puke. A scarlet light filtered out from underneath a closed door to her left. Low, muted groans came from behind a door to her right. She pulled on her yellow gloves and opened the right door.

The room wasn't very big, but it didn't need to be. Work with what you have, that was Kelly's motto. And the space she had was plenty.

Fake wood panels lined the four walls. They were a crude impersonation of mahogany, but they did a good job of covering up the acoustic foam. Plus, they were much easier to disinfect than real wood. A grid of linoleum tiles made up the floor. The polyvinyl squares had once been wall-to-wall carpet the color of moss, but once Kelly started to explore new hobbies, it was obvious the carpet had to go.

Power tools of all varieties were spread out on the two metal workbenches that flanked the large table in the middle of the room. Strapped onto the central table was a man. His arms and legs were tied down and drenched with sweat. A cloth around his mouth subdued his screams. He should have realized no one was coming for him by then, but that didn't stop him from exhausting his vocal cords.

Kelly put her things down on one of the tables and approached the man. Tenderly, she removed the cloth from his mouth. He tried to yell, but only a pitiful croak escaped his chapped lips. Kelly selected a nail gun and loaded it with three rusty nails.

"I'm going to ask you three questions," she said. "For each one you answer correctly, I'll drive one nail into your left thigh with this," she gestured to the gun. "For each question you answer incorrectly, however, I'll drive one nail into your right thigh using this." She picked up a hammer. "You can tell me which one hurts more."

The man's bloodshot eyes widened. "No, please don't do this," he whimpered.

"First question. Have you ever done anything wrong in your life?"

"Please let me go. I won't tell anyone, just let me go, please."

A muscle in Kelly's neck twitched. "Answer the question."

"No! I haven't done anything wrong, ever, I promise."

Kelly scoffed. "Fine, I guess we're doing this the hard way."

She held a rusty nail loosely between her fingers and balanced it on Mr. Miller's leg. With her other hand she grabbed a hammer and held it over the nail. She gave it three short, forceful taps.

"Stop! Stop! Please!"

Kelly raised her arm and slammed the hammer onto the nail. The metal drove into the bone with a thud and disappeared into Mr. Miller's flesh. A guttural scream ripped from his throat and he thrashed against his bonds.

"Incorrect. Do not lie to me, Mr. Miller," she chided.

His breath came in short, nervous gasps. "How do you know my name?"

"I know everything there is to know about you, Mr. Miller. You live at 52 Begonia Drive, you drive a Honda, you go to the grocery store every Tuesday at nine in the morning, your mother's name is Charlotte, and you donate to charity during the holidays. But you, Mr. Miller, are not a good person."

His lip quivered, wet with sweat and drool. "Please, you don't have to do this."

"Is that what the Walker family said when you killed them?"

Mr. Miller blinked. "What?"

"The Walker family. They lived not three miles from here. Did they beg for their lives as desperately as you are right now? Did they scream as loudly as you? Did you watch the life drain from their eyes when you brutally murdered them?"

Tears streamed down his face and snot dribbled from his nose. "How do you know that?"

Kelly leaned in close until she could smell the sour fear on his breath. "I told you: I know everything there is to know about you, Mr. Miller. Question number two: Are those tears for the Walkers or for yourself?"

A dark stain spread below his belt and the stench of urine filled the room. "They…they're for the Walkers," he stammered.

"Incorrect. They—"

Kelly's cell phone vibrated against her leg.

"One moment, please." She turned away and pulled out her phone. An unfamiliar number flashed on the screen, labeled as an unknown caller. She swiped it away and put her phone in her pocket.

"Sorry about that. As I was saying: incorrect. Those tears are not for the Walkers, they're for yourself. You're terrified of what I'm going to do to you now that you've had a taste."

"No, please, don't do it, don't do it—"

He howled and strained against the straps holding him down as another rusty nail disappeared into his thigh with a squelch. Blood soaked through his pants.

"Does your regret or self-pity bring you more pain?" she wondered aloud. "Perhaps they're equally painful?"

He didn't respond.

"Tell me, Mr. Miller, why did you do it? Why did you kill those people?"

He glared at her. Fury flashed over his face. "I'll tell you why. I killed those bastards because I could. That's all it was. I didn't even know them, but I ended their lives. It felt good. I wanted to do it. And I'd do it again—"

Kelly's phone buzzed.

"Sorry, hold that thought." Kelly reached into her pocket and turned off her phone.

Mr. Miller spat in her face. "No. I'm done with this. If you're gonna kill me, then do it you crazy bitch. You think you're scary? When I get outta here, what I did to the Walkers won't mean shit compared to what I'll do to you. You think you're tough shit, but at the end of the day, you aren't gonna kill me. You don't have the guts."

"I don't have the guts, huh?" Kelly shrugged. "If you say so." Metal glinted in the dim light as she raised the hammer above his head.

Mr. Miller's eyes grew wide, darting around frantically. "Wait, no. No!"

Kelly brought the hammer down on his head. She struck him again and again until his head caved in like a smashed pumpkin. Mr. Miller's skull gave way with a sickening *crack* to reveal bone and brain. The soft gray matter squished into mushy pulp that flung off the hammer claw in globs on each swing. His nose crumpled inward and his eyeballs popped like peeled grapes. Hot blood splattered Kelly's face and the taste of iron was sharp on her tongue.

When he was dead, she pulled out her phone and put on her favorite playlist. "Oops!…I Did It Again" by Britney Spears blasted through the speakers in the basement. Kelly grabbed a saw from the table and the circular blade whirred to life. She guided it toward the meatiest part of his thigh and squinted through the torrent of red that sprayed up once the blade made contact. The whirling edge sliced through fat and muscle like butter and slowed at the bone. Ligaments and tendons snapped like twigs with horrible, unforgettable cracks.

As Kelly set the saw at the hip, her phone rang. She jerked and the blade split open Mr. Miller's abdomen. His intestines burst out of the abdominal cavity under the pressure, juicier than rotten fruit. Kelly squealed and fumbled to turn off the saw.

"Gross," she whined, shaking clumps of gore from her hands. She held the saw in one hand and wiped off the other to turn down the music and answer the phone. It was the same number from before.

"Hello?"

"You were right, Kelly, you do have a lovely home," said a familiar voice.

She grinned. "I'm so glad you like it. Have you seen the basement yet? Why don't you come down?" Kelly opened the door to the stairwell.

A series of creaking noises came from the phone.

"Kelly, I hope you've said your goodbyes…what the hell?"

A tall, hooded figure loomed in the doorway holding a knife. They wore a long black cloak and a red plastic mask. The hem of their cloak and their boots were caked in mud.

Kelly sighed. "I could forgive the harassing phone calls and the home invasion, but I draw the line at tracking mud through my freshly cleaned house."

The intruder glanced at the dismembered corpse on the table, the pool of blood on the floor, and Kelly, saw in hand.

Begonia Drive was not known for its flowers.

"So sorry to intrude. I understand why you didn't want to talk before…"

Huh. I guess it wasn't punk kids after all. Kelly powered up the saw.

The stranger backed up. "I'll leave now. I didn't see anything…"

Work with what you have, that was Kelly's motto.

About the Authors

Amber Bliss (Editor) holds an MFA in Writing Popular Fiction from Seton Hill University and an MLIS from the University of Rhode Island. With a combination of creativity, determination, and a little sorcery, she's managed to combine her passion for writing and tabletop RPGs into her work as a librarian. Amber's days are consumed by stories, whether she's writing them, reading them, or telling them around a table cluttered with dice and character sheets because stories don't only make us werewolves and wizards, they make us human. Her own work can be found in *The Monstrous Feminine* by Scary Dairy Press. You can visit Amber at www.amberbliss.com or follow her @am_bliss on Twitter.

Lou Blair (ey/em/eir) is a queer, trans, and demi writer and linguist who moved to Providence because of a pop punk song. Originally from Seattle, Providence is the sixth city and third state capital ey have called home. Lou writes queer sci-fi/fantasy, contemporary Achillean romance, and once a piece of *Baby Driver/Dirty Dancing* fanfiction. Ey spend eir free time constructing languages, going to indie bookstores, and wrangling eir two cats.

Sarah DeCataldo's love of writing extends back to elementary school. Whether it was poems, song lyrics, stories, or research papers, Sarah was, and still is, always writing. By trade, Sarah is a nonprofit consultant, helping community organizations with raising funds and awareness to support their important work. She is also an adjunct professor in the Criminal Justice Department at Johnson & Wales University, a board member of SAGE-RI, and a steering committee member of 100 Women Who Care RI. In addition to writing and community work, Sarah enjoys being outdoors, drinking coffee, dancing, and playing the drums. Sarah lives in Cranston with her wife Tara and their fur-son Snoop. They hope to retire in Hawaii one day.

A.M.H. Devine resides in Providence with their found family and their beloved dog. On any given day you can find them poking mushrooms in the woods, drinking hot chocolate, or picking up a new hobby. Their work has previously been published in *Mad Scientist Journal*.

Theresa Katin lives in Portsmouth, Rhode Island with her family. Fortunately, she does not reside on Begonia Drive. She enjoys writing a variety of speculative fiction with soft spots for horror and poetry. Her passions include theater, music, books, television, and movies. You can contact her through her email katintc19@gmail.com.

C. H. Kim is a green-thumbed educator who found it entirely too easy to justify moving from California to Rhode Island. They use the notes app on their phone to document story ideas, doomsday plans, their partner's baking endeavors (a list named "Carbie Heaven"), and potential names for future pet chickens. While this is their first publication, they hope to continue provoking readers with more stories about the weird, wide world around us. You can reach them at rainbowquiche@gmail.com

Nathan Moone is a Writing and Psychology double major at Ithaca College. He was born in West Warwick, Rhode Island where he was able to have his first publication in the anthology *Voices of the Lost Year*. Nathan is a proud pansexual individual who loves giving his puppies belly rubs and exploring his voice in the writing world.

K. Parr is a writer of multiple genres, including young adult, romance, fantasy, paranormal, and humor, all of which star LGBTQ+ characters. She received her MFA in Writing Popular Fiction from Seton Hill University in 2017, and currently works as a teen librarian in Rhode Island. In her spare time, she reads and writes fanfiction, keeps up with way too many TV shows, and loves poking fun at her favorite tropes. You can follow her at:

Website: https://www.kparrbooks.com/
Facebook: https://www.facebook.com/authorkparr
Twitter: @kparrbooks
Instagram: @authorkparr

Charles Reis was born and raised in Coventry, Rhode Island, but currently lives in neighboring West Warwick. The proud New Englander graduated from the University of Rhode Island with a BA in English Literature in 2012 and currently works as a museum tour guide. Works of his have appeared in *One Night in Salem*, *More Lore for the Mythos*, and *Cursed*. You can follow Charles at:

Facebook: https://www.facebook.com/charles.reis.35
Instagram: @cthulhudawn1979

Linkedin: https://www.linkedin.com/in/charles-reis-a4597979/

Lauren Starnino is a fan of all things horror, and is a massive book, music and movie nerd. She writes short fiction as well as trivia. In 2017 she married the girl of her dreams. Lauren and Megan live with their orange cat, Finley. All 3 were born and raised in RI.